PRAISE

"A fast-paced, sexy novella for anyone looking for a fun, romantic read!"

-Rebecca Hefner, author of The End of Hatred

"The bear shifter romance you didn't know you needed!"

- Kate, @kate_reads_

"I just found this book so entertaining. It was exactly what I needed on a hard day, and I would gladly read more..."

- Corey Alexander, Corey's Book Corner

I couldn't get enough of the heat between this growly bear shifter and his city-girl mate. I read it twice in one week!Funny. Steamy. Growly. Full circle satisfying.

- Eve Kasey, author of Love in Stone

PRAISE FOR LUCY EDEN

EVERYTHING'S BETTER WITH YOU

"Everything's Better With You is a rare gem in the romance novel world. It has depth, great characters and a totally believable story line."

- The Laundry Librarian

EVERYTHING'S BETTER WITH KIMBERLY

"Engaging with attention to detail and kept me hooked from start to finish."

- Janine Caroline, Author of *I Look at You and Smile*

CHERISHING THE GODDESS

"The perfect balance of humor, angst, and steam. Highly recommended!"

- PE Kavanaugh, Author of *Sex, Money and the Price of Truth*

"This enemies to lovers romance will make your insides roar and you will want to pick up Lucy Eden's backlist immediately."

- Silvana Reyes, Frolic Media

ALSO BY LUCY EDEN

DON'T MISS MY NEXT RELEASE!

Sign up for my newsletter for updates & freebies.

VISIT LUCYEDEN.COM

COPYRIGHT

CONTENTS

Every story is for my mom, who made me fall in love with reading & Ms. K, who made me fall in love with writing.

BEAR WITH ME

Hi, I'm Celestine Woods. Most people call me Chellie.

If you are one of my 850K followers, you might know me as the super successful influencer, but more than likely you probably know me as the woman who had an alcohol-fueled meltdown at the biggest New Year's Eve party in the world after getting dumped by her former rock star boyfriend, who then publicly professed his love for his new girlfriend in a song, before getting engaged a week later.

So, I went to Black Bear Mountain, a cabin resort in the Catskill Mountains, to relax, recharge, rehab my image and toss in a couple sponsored posts. The only hitch in my plan for R&R is the sexy, but grumpy, lumberjack who runs the place. His people skills leave a lot to be desired and it's no wonder I'm the only guest. His resort and my image could both use a little TLC, so we formed a truce and teamed up to help each other.

My social media know-how, my smartphone, a gorgeous grumpy mountain man and a strangely friendly bear that keeps coming to my window every night is the perfect recipe for project #ChellieIn-TheWoods?

*includes the paperback exclusive bonus epilogue, Grin & Bear it *

For Content Warnings for all my books, please visit:

LUCYEDEN.COM/CW

BEAR WITH ME

LUCY EDEN

HAPPY NEW YEAR!

"**O**h my God, Chellie. Are you still listening to that song?" My roommate, Dawn, stomped over to my laptop and slammed it shut. It was a stupid question because the song she was asking about blared from my computer's speakers, so obviously, I was still listening to it.

"Hey!" I tried to reopen my laptop, but she snatched it off of my bed and clutched it to her chest.

"Chellie, this is ridiculous. You've been in bed for two days. I know you're upset. But torturing yourself by listening to a song your ex wrote for his new girl-friend is not going to make you feel better. He's not thinking about you, so you need to stop thinking about him."

"Brutal, Dawn." I grabbed my comforter and pulled it over my head. She tugged it down.

"No, you're getting out of this bed."

"Why are you doing this? You know what Mike did to me. My Instagram comments are a mess. Forget about my Twitter mentions. My manager is going apeshit... Just, please, let me be sad."

"No." She flopped onto my bed next to me and lay down, boring into me with her dark brown eyes. "Your job is sharing your life, right?"

I nodded. I was a social media influencer. I posted about my life, and I partnered with brands to expose followers to exciting products and experiences for a fee.

"Well, girl. This is your life. Share it." She snatched my phone off of the nightstand. "You're not the first person to get dumped. I'm not saying you can't be sad, but pathetic is definitely not your brand."

"Since when do you care about my brand?"

"Since you pay half the rent and utilities and have no other discernible skills." She smirked at me.

"I thought you hated my job."

She rolled over to face me and sighed.

"I don't hate your job. I hate that you portray this ridiculous unattainable lifestyle that your followers think they can emulate if they buy the shit you shill. Your life is nothing like this." She held up my phone. "And you kill yourself to pretend that it is. You don't even use half the shit you post about."

I sat up.

"That's not true. I personally test every product before I agree to post about it. Why do you think I won't post that diet tea?"

Dawn snorted laughter.

"Oh my God! That tea that gave you diarrhea?" She laughed again, and I joined her. "Weren't you at a party when it kicked in?"

"Yes. It was so embarrassing. I didn't make it to the bathroom in time. I had to throw away a Halston Heritage romper, wear Mike's coat and sneak out through the kitchen." Mike took me home, fed me copious amounts of soup, and sat outside the bathroom door for hours. The memory of the way he took care of me that night hit me harder than I thought it would. I leaned back into my bed and tugged at my comforter again.

"My point is that your look and lifestyle are unattainable for most people. You shouldn't be ashamed of it, but you should be honest about how you got it. If authenticity and honesty really is your brand, start today." She pointed to my phone before turning on her heel and leaving my bedroom, grabbing my laptop on her way out.

I heaved a deep sigh, got out of bed, and padded to my vanity. Jesus Christ, I looked terrible.

I washed my face, brushed my teeth, sprinkled some dry shampoo in my hair, ran a brush through it, and slathered my face with about twenty dollars' worth of *Le Oceanoa* soothing gel moisturizer. I definitely looked better, but I topped off my no-makeup look with a coat of mascara, highlighting cream on my cheeks and a little bit of gloss. I took a deep cleansing breath, clipped the selfie ring light to my phone, and smiled.

When I finally chose the perfect sad but strong selfie, I typed a caption.

chelliewoods: Hey, loves! Today is another day. I'm still so sad, but I'm determined to not let my life be ruled by the decisions of others. You shouldn't either. Life has ups and downs, but don't let it get you down. Get up, wash your face, and take on the day like the warrior you are. But don't forget to moisturize!

BTW, New Year's is around the corner. What are some of your resolutions? I'm thinking about saving some money by canceling my @spotify account. (Winking face emoji) JK! Love you, Spotify! (Kissing face emoji)

#Breakupselfie #sadbutstrong #nofilter #nomakeup #allaboutmygirls #loveyourselfalways #laoceanoa #ad

I stared at the caption for a minute, feeling my stomach doing flips. My heart began to race. I hit the send button and squeezed my eyes shut. I sucked in a deep breath and slowly opened them. I stared at the post.

In fifteen seconds, I'd accumulated 146 likes. I refreshed again. 623 likes and a comment:

stacidances sooooooo pretty! (Heart emoji)

I refreshed again. In less than a minute I'd accumulated over 2,000 likes and more comments:

ester.jakes you look good, girl. I wished I looked that good after my breakup.

candi.martinez453 love you, Chellie!! (Cherry blossom emoji)

waist.trainr.427 Get snatched for Valentine's Day!!! Use my promo code for 50% off. Link in my bio!

hollyhollywood killin' it, love!!!!

I KEPT REFRESHING. The likes and comments kept climbing, flooding my body with a warm sense of relief and feeling of purpose. Sure, there were a couple of trolls and assholes, but the ratio was definitely in my favor. I'd been staring at my account for over thirty minutes when my manager called.

"HEY, BRENDA! WHAT'S UP?" I put her on speaker-phone so I could continue to scroll. 27k likes and counting. Thirty thousand likes in a half hour was high for me, and I guessed that's why she was calling.

"Don't what's up me. You know you should have cleared that sponsored post with me." She paused for a second. "But you're lucky because it's going viral and *Le Oceanoa* loves it. I'm getting calls and emails. Offers, girl, big ones!"

"That's crazy! What kind of offers?"

"The Kick wants you to host their New Year's Eve Party. They're paying five figures, and you only have to be there for two hours. It will be a great opportunity for the world to see you back to yourself, and I can probably work in some good sponsorship opportunities: dress, jewelry, shoes, blah, blah, blah..."

"Bren, New Year's Eve is in five days. I'm not sure..."

"You *are* ready," she said, accurately reading my mind. "It's been over a week, and yes, your boyfriend broke up with you but suck it up, buttercup. People break up in public all the time and survive. You want to be a celebrity. This is part of it."

"Okay." I sighed. "I'll do it."

"And, Chellie," she added. "Delete the 'no makeup' hashtag and tag the makeup brands you used."

"But I didn't—" My words died abruptly as Brenda interrupted.

"Don't test me. I'm still visiting my family for the holidays, and there is not enough coffee or wine in the world to help me put up with their bullshit *and* yours. Fix it."

"Fine." I nodded and ended the call.

———— • • • • ————

THE KICK WAS a lifestyle and media website that was worth billions, and every year, rented a five-star luxury hotel in a different city to throw their New Year's Eve Party. This year was New York, and I was chosen, at the last minute, to host with over a dozen other influencers and celebrities, each of us assigned to our sections of the party. Dawn was my date.

I was hosting the Female Empowerment party, which had Dawn rolling her eyes so hard I thought they might pop out of her head. The DJ was a woman, playing mostly women-created music along with serving pink cocktails. Admittedly, it was pretty terrible, and I would have bet my appearance fee that a man put this together. The word "female" was a dead giveaway.

The night was going well, and I actually managed to forget about Mike for a while. Every once in a while, someone would approach me to tell me how brave I was for going outside and that Mike would come crawling back. I doubted the truth in either of these. I pasted on smiles to cover my sadness and laughed to stop myself from crying.

Midnight came and went. I counted down to midnight and watched the confetti and balloons fall. Dawn even stopped babysitting me and let herself relax, enjoying about three pink cocktails.

About forty-five minutes into 2019, I whipped out my phone and took a selfie with the party below the VIP balcony as a backdrop.

chelliewoods Happy 2019! Love you all, you gorgeous warriors! Xoxo Chellie!

#HappyNewYear #LoveYourself

I refreshed. 125 likes. I refreshed again. 372 likes, and the comments started.

thotsrus omg! She doesn't know!

Long.azz.hair OMG! These hair vitamins are the best I've tried. My hair grew 6 inches in 2 months!!!! Use my promo code for 25% off. Link in my bio.

Kimmit002 don't let that man get you down. You'll find someone better.

xena.gregg Damn, that ring is pitiful!!! You dodged a bullet, boo.

thirsttrapmike so you single, boo? Check your DMs, gorgeous. (eggplant emoji) (eggplant emoji) (eggplant emoji)

What the hell was going on? Ring? My heart started pounding. I opened my browser and searched for Mike. The first headline caught my eye:

Has Grammy-winning, former rocker Mike Duke, found true love just a week after ditching Instagram model Celestine Woods?

I scrolled, skimming the article until I saw the photo. It was a woman's hand that I assumed was Jane's wearing a plain thin gold band with a gold star. She apparently posted it in her private Instagram account, but someone must have leaked it.

There's no way that's an engagement ring.

That's terrible, even for Mike. But it was perfect for Jane. She would probably love a ring like that. The whole time I knew her, I don't think I've ever seen her wear any jewelry.

To the left of it was the photo I posted on Instagram the day before Mike dumped me. It was a selfie of Mike and me posing in front of Christmas gifts we'd spent the entire morning wrapping for homeless kids. Of course, Jane was there. It was her idea. I stared at the photo, scrutinizing Mike's face for any clue that he was planning to end things. There was nothing.

Then it hit me.

Mike dumped me after a year with no warning. Now he's engaged to someone else. My chest felt like it was being crushed. My dress, my shoes—hell, everything I was wearing felt too tight. I wanted to escape, but it was too early to leave the party.

I signaled our server to bring me three pink drinks. I gulped them down and started to relax. I ordered three more. I remembered the server lowering the tray on my table with the new trio of drinks, but I didn't remember anything after that.

2

DEATH SUCKING ON A LIFESAVER

I woke up at three o'clock in the afternoon on January 1st. I reached for my phone, but it was nowhere around. My heart started pounding, and I sat up to search for it. When I did, my head felt like someone was kicking it from the inside, so I laid back down. There was a huge glass of water by my bedside and two Advil on a napkin. I swallowed them and chased them with the water before crawling under the sheets.

There was a knock on my door. I'd meant to yell, "come in," but what erupted from my mouth sounded like a zombie moan. Dawn poked her head in, and her body followed once she saw I was awake.

"Where's my phone?" I croaked. Dawn just shook her head.

"Does that mean you don't know where my phone is, or does that mean you're not going to give it to me?"

"The last thing you need is to look at your phone," she said. I glanced around my bedroom. "That also goes for your laptop and your tablet." She added, correctly reading my mind. "This is a technology-free zone...for now."

"Dawn, stop fucking around. Technology is my job..." My words died away at the look on her face. "What?"

She walked over to my bed and sat down. "How much of last night do you remember?" Her expression had me worried, but I tried to tune out the pounding of my head and focus. Last night felt like a black hole in my memory. Then certain parts gained color, and the blurred edges sharpened.

"Mike's engaged." I sighed.

"What do you remember about the party?"

I sighed again and tried to focus.

"We counted down to midnight. There were balloons and confetti. I found out my ex-boyfriend of two weeks is getting married to someone else. I had a couple drinks..." That's when the memories ended. Dread crept over me, causing my stomach to churn. Nothing good ever started with, "*I had a couple of drinks, and then I don't remember anything...*"

"Oh my God! What happened?"

"I'm not sure exactly." Dawn wore an expression that looked like guilt. "I'd met a friend, and we were *talking* when my phone started blowing up with alerts." She stopped speaking.

"Dawn. Keep saying words."

She put her hand over mine. "You started posting on Instagram."

That doesn't sound that bad. I can talk my way out of a few drunk pics. I was at a New Year's Eve party, right?

"They were videos. Three of them actually."

My body deflated, and I let out a sound that was a cross between a sigh and a whimper. "Were they bad?"

She nodded. "The first two were about Mike, and the third one was you making out with a stranger. I managed to stop you before you made a fourth one. There's also a fair amount of drunken selfies with 'fans' and a few videos of the hotel's security carrying you out of the party.

Oh my God. Oh my fucking God.

"You threw up on one of them, but he didn't get too upset. Eric helped me get you inside, and you threw up on him too." Eric was one of the doormen/security guards for our building.

My eyes welled up with tears.

"Did Brenda call?"

"Yes, everyone has called. Your grandmother called. She's the only person I would've let you talk to, but she insisted I let you sleep. The phone will not stop ringing. That's why I took it away." She sighed and placed her hand on my thigh over my duvet. "Mike is here."

"What?" I sat up, and my head started ringing again. "I don't want to see him. Did you tell him that I didn't want to see him?"

"He wanted to make sure that you were okay."

I've only been awake for an hour, and 2019 is already shaping up to be the worst year of my life.

"He also said he wanted to apologize."

Apologize? Now, I was curious.

"How do I look?" I tried to smooth my hair away from my face before turning to face Dawn.

"Like death sucking on a lifesaver." She tried to stifle a smile before she walked to my bathroom and rolled my makeup cart to my beside. "How long you need?"

"Five minutes should be fine." I glanced at my hand mirror.

Holy Fuck. I did look like death sucking on a lifesaver. How drunk was I that I went to bed without removing my makeup?

"Ten minutes! I need ten minutes."

————— •••• —————

TWENTY MINUTES LATER, I gave Dawn the signal. She left my room, then the tall, bearded asshole who ruined my life entered. He ducked his head into my room, wearing a sheepish half smile and holding a white paper bag with huge grease spots on the bottom. I crossed my arms and tilted my chin upwards, trying my best to look regal and indignant, but the sight of the bag and the familiar smell that emanated from it made my traitorous stomach growl.

Mike walked in and took a seat in my armchair. The last time he sat in that chair, we were naked, and I was straddling him. That was last summer, then I realized that Mike and I hadn't had sex in months. Maybe that was something I should have paid attention to. I bet he doesn't have that problem now. I pursed my lips.

With my head tilted and eyebrows raised, I flicked a glance at the bag he was holding. He leaned forward, and I snatched it from his hand.

I stuck my face in the bag and inhaled. My favorite hangover remedy was inside, and one of my few indulgences. I didn't eat ice cream. In fact, I avoided carbs and sugar like the plague, and I didn't drink to excess. However, the few times I did, I allowed myself to indulge in a triple hefty burger from Bubba's Burger Joint with cheddar, Swiss and jack cheeses, double bacon, special sauce, and onion rings. I tore open the burger's wrapping and took a bite. Shuddering, I closed my eyes. It was so good. Mike was watching me with a smug look of amusement. I should have thanked him, but instead, I said, "You forgot the onion rings."

"Nope," he replied. "They're in there."

"They're in the bag, but you're supposed to ask for onion rings on the burger, so they soak up the special sauce."

"You're right." He chuckled and sat back in the chair. "I'm sorry."

Speaking of sorry.

"Why are you here?" I asked through a mouthful of burger.

His smile faded, he wiped his hands over his face and tugged on his beard.

"Look, I didn't handle this the best way. Something happened, and it made me realize that my life wasn't going the way I wanted it to, and I needed to fix it. We weren't happy, and it wasn't fair to either of us to keep pretending but—"

"Stop. Your *'it's not you, it's me'* speech sucked the first time. I don't want to hear it again." I took another bite of my burger and shoved an onion ring in my mouth. He nodded and sighed.

"I'm sorry about the song and the engagement. All of that shit was supposed to be private. I should've been more careful. I didn't mean to hurt you."

I stopped chewing for a moment because a lump had formed in my throat, and my chest constricted at Mike's words.

"What makes you think you hurt me?"

He averted his eyes and started picking at a piece of lint on his jeans.

"I saw the videos."

I stopped chewing again.

"Judging by the look on your face, you haven't seen them and don't remember what you said..." He looked at me, and I looked away, shaking my head. "Or did?"

"Dawn gave me the gist."

"Chellie, I didn't come here for forgiveness. I don't deserve it. I just wanted to make sure you were okay and to let you know that none of this was intentional." He got quiet for a while. "I also wanted to give you this." He held out what looked like a brochure. I sucked the special sauce off of my fingers and snatched it out of his hand. There was a picture of a log cabin, and it was surrounded by trees. This brochure looked like it was designed before I was born and printed on a home computer. There wasn't even a website.

"What is this?"

"A guy I went to high school with owns a bunch of cabins in the woods. He rents them out. It's a good place to unwind and regroup. It might be good for you to get away for a while. Let everything blow over. It's all paid for, whenever you want to go."

"Are you fucking kidding me? You're trying to send me away?" I tossed the brochure at him. "What? Are you and Jane planning a parade down Fifth Avenue?" Her name tasted like ash in my mouth.

"No," he groaned. "I'm just trying to help."

"Well, you've been *very* helpful this last week." I said sarcastically. "Thank you for *all* the helping. Now, you can help me by getting out."

Mike put his hands on his knees and rose to leave. He picked up the brochure and put it on my bedside table.

He pulled the door open and turned to look at me.

"Just think about it, Chell. I really do care about you, and I am really sorry. I just want you to be okay."

I didn't respond. Even though I was furious at Mike and probably would be for a long time, I knew he was right. We would have broken up eventually, but that didn't make my current situation—that he caused—any easier. Throwing my burger and hitting him in his stupid chiseled face would have made me feel better, but I was too hungry. I just watched him leave and ate another onion ring.

———— ···· ————

DAWN CAME INTO MY ROOM, holding my phone.

Thank God.

I sucked the sauce off my fingers and made grabby hands at her.

She held my precious out to me, then swung it out of my reach when I went to grab for it.

"Your mom's on the phone. I'm taking it back as soon as you're done."

She wasn't backing down from my glares. I nodded and held my hand out again.

"Hello, Mother."

Dawn occupied the seat Mike just vacated.

"Chellie Belly, what a mess!" My mother set the tone for our conversation by using my childhood nickname alluding to my childhood weight issues, which my therapist tells me are really her issues. "What were you thinking?"

"I wasn't thinking, Mother. I was drunk," I replied deadpan. I noticed Dawn stifle a smile, and it cheered me up a little.

"I just got off the phone with Brenda. She says you're not answering her calls?"

"Nope. I'm hungover, and Dawn is holding my phone hostage."

"It figures. I swear that girl is jealous of you. I heard she was also at the party with you. She was a big help, wasn't she?" My mother wasn't fond of Dawn, and the feeling was mutual. I was on #TeamDawn.

"What do you want?"

"I want you to talk to your manager and figure out how to sort out this mess. The girl I raised does not run away from her responsibilities."

Although I was raised by nannies, I wouldn't mention it because I wanted to get her off of the phone as soon as possible.

"Okay. I'll call Brenda. I have to go. I'm in the middle of eating."

"I hope you're not eating one of those disgusting burgers."

"Nope. Fruit salad." I shoved another onion ring in my mouth.

"Good, but not too much fruit. It's full of sugar." She sighed. "I could wring Mike's neck for embarrassing you like this. You're good to be rid of him. Did you see that ring? Did he find it in a Cracker Jack box? And I heard this new girl of his is homely. Have you met her?"

"No, I haven't." Actually, I'd met Jane dozens of times throughout my relationship with Mike, and she was far from homely. She'd be prettier if she made an effort, but I wasn't ready to talk about Jane to anyone, much less my mother, who at the moment seemed more concerned about mending my career rather than my possibly broken heart. My phone beeped, indicating that I had a call coming in. It was from Brenda. I didn't want to talk to her, but I wanted to talk to my mother even less. "That's Brenda. I have to go."

"Okay, Chellie Belly. Let me know how it goes and be sure to get some exercise. The endorphins will be good for you."

"Okay."

Bye, Mommy. Love you too!

I rolled my eyes and answered Brenda's call.

"Hi, Brenda." I tried to sound cheerful.

"Don't you *Hi, Brenda* me. What the actual fuck was that?"

"I'm sorry, but I told you that I wasn't ready. I—"

"Oh, grow the fuck up, Chellie. Your sponsors are dropping like flies, and The Kick is refusing to pay your appearance fee. They've threatened to sue."

"I thought you said all publicity was good publicity."

"That's bullshit unless you want to accept the three very lucrative offers I've gotten from porn companies." She paused for effect, and it worked. I got quiet. While I have nothing against porn—I watch quite a bit of it—doing porn wasn't in my five-year plan. "We need to figure out a way to rehab your image fast or you're finished. You have the *just dumped* pity thing working for you, but that's only gonna last so long before people get bored. So, you better come up with something fast."

My gaze fell upon the picture of the log cabin.

Damn it.

"Actually." I snatched the brochure off of my nightstand and turned it over in my hand, rolling my eyes while cursing Mike's existence. "I have an idea."

3

SERIAL KILLERS ARE ALWAYS
CHARMING

"You know this doesn't look anything like the brochure."

Dawn was right, of course, but I was trying to remain optimistic. This was my chance to rehab my image without actually having to go to rehab. Plus, I'd already sold the idea to Brenda and started posting about it online.

Brenda was beside herself with excitement. *Project: Chellie in the Woods* was precisely what I needed to get back in the game. I would be spending a month embracing nature, self-healing, and of course, partnering with about a dozen brands to promote everything from bamboo yoga mats to solar-powered kettles. I didn't know how to use half of the stuff that was loaded into the trunk of the SUV that carried us four hours away from the city and into the Catskill Mountains, but I was smart, resourceful, and frankly desperate.

Dawn came with me to help me get settled, but she could only stay for the weekend. Our driver helped us load our luggage into the house and left us to our own devices.

"Tomorrow at six o'clock, right, Frank?" Dawn called after him.

"Yes, ma'am," he replied before slamming the door and backing out of the gravel driveway.

"Girl, are you sure about this?" Dawn eyed me warily as we stepped into the living room. The cabin wasn't that bad. It needed a good cleaning, a better decorator—my thoughts were interrupted by a noise behind us, but when we looked, there was nothing— and maybe an exorcism.

"Yes, I'm sure. There's heat, hot water, electricity, and the most important thing, high-speed internet. It'll be fine."

"Hmm," Dawn huffed, not convinced.

We explored the house. It was larger than it looked from the outside. There were two bedrooms, a kitchen, a full bathroom, and a large main room with a fireplace. All it needed was a bearskin rug.

We were unpacking groceries when a knock on the door made us jump.

"Are you expecting anyone?" Dawn asked. I tilted my head and pursed my lips in answer to her ridiculous question.

"Well then, who the hell is that? I'm not answering the door."

"Tanner," a deep muffled voice called from outside to answer her question. "I'm Mike's friend. I own the cabin. I came to see if you were settling in okay or if you needed anything..."

"Chellie, how much of that man's life story do you need to hear before you open the door?"

"Then, why don't you answer the door?" I whispered.

"This isn't my house." She stepped behind me and nudged me towards the door.

"Fine." I walked towards the door. There was no peephole, but I also realized that I had no idea what this Tanner guy looked like anyway.

"How do I know you're not an ax murderer?"

"What?" He laughed on the other side of the door.

"Seriously?" Dawn whispered.

"Well, I promise you I'm not an ax murderer, but that's probably something an ax murderer would say."

A chuckle I tried to stifle bubbled out of me, and that was a bad sign. I watched enough ID network to know that serial killers were always charming.

"What's your insta?"

"My what?"

"Your Instagram account. I'll look you up."

"I don't have an...Instagram account," he said. I shot Dawn a look of alarm.

"Twitter?"

"Nope."

"Snapchat?"

"You making up words?"

"Do you have a Facebook account?" My nana had a Facebook account.

"I did, but I deleted it years ago."

"Oh my God. He's definitely a psycho!" I whispered to Dawn.

"Hold on," he said through the door. There was a long pause before I felt my phone vibrate in my pocket. I pulled it out, and the word "dickhead" flashed across my screen.

"Mike?" I answered the phone.

"Hey, Tanner just called me. He said you're refusing to open the door, grilling him about social media, and you called him a psycho?" He laughed. I was glad Mike was enjoying himself while I was vetting possible serial killers in the cabin he sent me to in the middle of nowhere.

"First of all, stop laughing. Second of all, I'm not gonna open my door to random strangers in the woods. Who the hell doesn't have any social media accounts? And third of all, I didn't call him a psycho." *To his face. And how the hell did he hear me? I whispered it.*

"I'm sorry," he said through a chuckle and cleared his throat. "He's a good guy. I'm glad you decided to take me up on my offer."

"I didn't do it for you. I have to go." I ended the call.

I took a deep breath, smoothed my hair, and swept the door open.

"I'm sorry about that, I was just trying to be caref—" My breath was snatched from my throat along with my words. Tanner was gorgeous. Our eyes met, and something electric seemed to flicker between us, making my heart pound, and I was momentarily light-headed, but it was fleeting. He pinned me with an expression I couldn't identify, and it caused my entire body to ignite, but it was gone in an instant. What took its place was a look of pure annoyance. His annoyance annoyed me. I had a perfectly logical reaction to a stranger knocking on my door in the middle of the mountains. I could only attribute my initial response to him to not having sex for God knows how long. Did I mention that Tanner was really gorgeous?

He looked like Chris Hemsworth and Jason Momoa had a baby with the Brawny paper towel guy. And he was a giant. He towered over me, and I was 5'10. He was also wide, though that could have just been the giant coat he was wearing. It was the middle of winter, and we were in the mountains, and, oh shit, I'd left him out in the cold while I stared at him. I stepped aside to let him in. A gust of freezing wind followed him into the cabin.

He walked past me towards a giant coatrack. When his back was turned, I looked at Dawn. Her eyes were wide as saucers, and her jaw was on the ground.

"*Day-yum!*" she mouthed silently at me.

"*I know!*" I mouthed back.

He removed his coat and hung it on the rack. He turned to face us wearing a flannel shirt tucked into jeans that highlighted his thighs and ass a little too well. He raised his arms.

"See?" he replied deadpan. "No ax." He didn't smile, but he walked around the perimeter of the room, checking the windows.

Dawn and I glanced at each other and shrugged. I wasn't about to let Mr. Sexy Lumberjack make me feel bad about not wanting to get hacked to death in the middle of the woods.

"You have enough food?"

That was a weird question.

"Um, I think so." I walked to the kitchen, but his long legs outpaced me, and he beat me to the fridge, opened it and inspected its contents. I was just about to tell him off for invading our privacy when he opened his mouth to speak.

"How long is this supposed to last?" He looked at me accusingly. I glanced at Dawn in confusion, and she shrugged again.

"A week. I guess..."

"This is not enough food for two people for a week."

What the hell was this guy's problem? I crossed my arms and glared at him.

"Well, Dawn is leaving tomorrow, and this is plenty of food for one person for a week," I told Detective Tanner of the Catskill Mountain Food Police. "I could probably make these last two weeks." I couldn't, but something about his He-Man act was pissing me off. Unfortunately, it didn't make him less attractive.

He glared at me like he wanted to argue, and a part of me wanted him to argue. Yelling at a giant bearded man would feel really good right now even if Tanner wasn't the giant bearded man I was pissed at. He eyed me for another second, and I crossed my arms and tilted my head, my eyebrows raised. Our host moved on to checking the cabinets, shaking his head at my kale chips and seaweed wraps before continuing to inspect the cabin. Finally, he made his way to the coatrack, slipping into his jacket before facing me.

"My number's on the notepad on the table, with the password for the internet. I live in the big cabin down the road," he said in a gruff voice. Then he left.

"What the hell was that?" I turned to face Dawn. "That was weird, right?"

"I don't know. I thought it was sweet."

"Are you kidding me?"

"He checked the cabin to make sure it was safe, and he wanted to make sure you had enough to eat."

"Would you think it was sweet if he *didn't* look like an extra from *Sons of Anarchy*?"

"Don't make me answer that." She grinned, and I snorted a laugh.

———— •••• ————

WE SPENT the rest of the night organizing and unpacking. Dawn also helped me style and shoot some pics for my feed. I planned to preschedule two weeks' worth of posts to get started and use the time to actually relax and post for the rest of the month at my leisure.

I couldn't stop thinking about Tanner, the grumpy lumberjack. He definitely wasn't a fan of mine and not because he didn't have social media. He couldn't have been that pissed that I wouldn't let him into the cabin until I verified that he wasn't a serial killer.

And did he inspect the refrigerators of all of his guests? If he did, it would explain why this place was so deserted. I wondered what his Yelp! rating was.

After we styled enough pictures for me to post at least once a day for two weeks, we decided to get ready for bed.

I agreed to let Dawn have the bigger of the two bedrooms for the night to thank her for coming with me, but when I came back from my shower, she was sitting on my bed in her pajamas with a scarf wrapped around her head. Her chestnut-colored skin was scrubbed clean of makeup and glistening. The eucalyptus smell in the room told me she helped herself to my nighttime moisturizer. She was also wearing her glasses, meaning she'd taken her contacts out.

"What are you doing?" I asked, wrapping my hair in a cotton t-shirt.

"I know you didn't think I was sleeping in this creepy cabin in the woods by myself." She snuggled under the covers and pulled out her phone. "What was the internet password again? We were so busy doing your stuff I never got to connect my phone." Well, I guessed the matter of sleeping arrangements was settled.

"Um, Uroday, Usterway...shit, I forgot. Hold on, I'll go look."

I pulled on my robe and walked into the living room towards the table with the notepad that held Tanner's number and the internet password. I snatched the pad off the table and looked at the password again.

Damn. I was close.

I heard a rustling outside the window. Like a dummy, I rushed forward to see what it was. Standing outside the living room window was a huge black bear. It stood on its hind legs, but when we locked eyes—I made eye contact with a giant bear—it dropped to all fours, making me jump away from the window. I squealed, using all the energy I had not to scream and scare Dawn even more than she already was, dropped the notepad, and hauled ass back to the bedroom.

"What the hell is wrong with you?" Dawn sat up.

"Nothing," I said, not wanting to frighten her. I could tell her that I saw a giant bear peering in our window, but I don't think she'd want to hear that for some reason the bear felt familiar like it knew me or something, but what the hell did I know about bears. It was awfully close to the house, and I was secretly grateful for Tanner checking and double-checking the door locks and windows.

"Well, did you get the password?"

I nodded and gave it to her. She typed it in.

"Are you sure you're okay with me sleeping in here?"

"Yep." I crawled in bed next to her, suddenly grateful for her presence and even more thankful that it was her idea to sleep in the same room so I wouldn't have to explain my change of heart.

"That's an interesting password. It sounds like Latin. Imma look it up real quick."

Dawn was such a nerd. She latched on to any bit of useless trivia and random fact. When I traveled to Iceland to work and invited her to come with me, she spent the six weeks before our trip learning to speak Icelandic for no reason, not to mention dragging me to the penis museum in Reykjavík.

"Ha!" she proclaimed triumphantly. "I was right. *Ursidae* is a Latin word."

"For what?" I asked, hoping to distract myself from what I saw outside our window.

"Bear."

4

YOU SHOULD SIT ON IT

Watching Dawn leave was bittersweet. We hugged about four times, every time she asked me if I was sure about staying in the woods. I told her that I was sure, and though I was partly lying through my teeth, a part of me was excited about the solitude.

Brenda approved every post, but not without reminding me to try to squeeze in some candids and a couple of videos. Followers hate a feed that's nothing but sponsored posts, and my fans were very invested in my "recovery."

I was outside attempting to assemble a tent from one of my sponsors when I caught sight of Tanner. He leaned against a nearby tree watching me struggle, clearly not amused. He pinned me with a gaze that momentarily made me feel like a child caught misbehaving. Already frustrated by this damn tent, the last thing I needed was Tanner's grumpy lumberjack routine.

I must have watched the stupid instructional video ten times, but the only thing I could do correctly was laying out the ground cloth. The "easy" collapsible tent poles kept getting tangled, and I couldn't get the stupid clips to attach to the poles. Every time I tried to pull the tent up into the dome shape that allegedly fit six people, the clips came apart, and the poles came flying out. The third time I tried, I actually managed to get tangled up in the tent, necessitating a rescue.

Tanner unzipped the "door" and lifted the canvas so I could crawl out.

"Need some help?" He glowered at me. I definitely needed help, and I would have been tempted to accept his offer to help if he wasn't so smug.

"No," I huffed out, climbing to my feet while avoiding his outstretched hand. "I almost had it that time."

"I saw that." His voice dripped with sarcasm.

"What are you doing here?" I asked to change the subject. For some reason, I was embarrassed as well as annoyed.

"I came to check on you." He was making no effort to hide his annoyance now. "And your friend," he added quickly, looking around for Dawn. "I went into town for supplies. There's a storm coming. I brought you some real groceries in case you ran out of rabbit food." He looked around the yard. "You need more firewood—"

"Dawn went back to the city earlier, so it's just me."

"You're here by yourself?" His eyes seemed to momentarily flash in anger, and he wore the same expression from yesterday while he examined my bare cabinets.

"Excuse me, are you this attentive to all of your guests?"

"The ones that need it." He looked disdainfully at my outfit. I could've dressed a little more warmly, but the stupid YouTube video for the tent was only seven minutes long, and I sweat easily. I was also fifteen feet from the front door. I was wearing yoga pants, shell-toed Adidas, a long-sleeved t-shirt, and a puffer vest. I did have a hat on, at least.

"Well, thank you for your *hospitality,* but I'm fine."

"I saw that too." He gestured to the pile of metal and canvas at our feet. "Why are you putting up a tent? Something wrong with the cabin?" He glanced towards the house.

"The cabin is fine." I sighed, now wondering how I would explain the absurdity of putting up a thin canvas tent in the middle of winter when I had a perfectly good heated house to sleep in. Tanner already thought I was an idiot. His opinion of me shouldn't have affected me, but it did for some reason. But, I wasn't going to let him make me feel bad about doing my job. It wasn't always glamorous, and sometimes it didn't make sense, but I was good at it.

"One of my sponsors is a tent manufacturer, and they're paying me to post about this tent. I wasn't actually planning to sleep in it." I glared at him and raised my eyebrows.

"Okay," he said, bending down and straightening out one of the flexible poles. "You post pictures of yourself using this tent." He grabbed the other pole and straightened it. "And then what?" He began clipping the canvas to the poles. "People buy them?" He gave the pole canvas combination a weird flick, and it popped into the dome shape that had eluded me for the last hour. I was annoyed at how quickly he managed to assemble the tent, and it made him even sexier, which was more annoying.

"Yeah," I whispered, "something like that."

He opened the door to the tent and crawled inside. The manufacturer advertised this as a six-man tent, but I was sure Tanner wasn't one of the men the designers envisioned. He held the flap open and looked at me with raised eyebrows. I rolled my eyes and ducked into the tent. I sat next to him and pulled my knees to my chest, wrapping my arms around my shins.

Once I'd stopped moving and wasn't sweating or swearing, I realized that it was freezing and I *was* improperly dressed for the weather. I would never admit it, though. I didn't have to because I felt myself being blanketed in warmth. Tanner had removed his thick winter coat and wrapped it around my shoulders.

I was too cold to be indignant, so I wrapped myself in it and tried to pretend not to be affected by Tanner's *man of the woods* smell. My body wasn't doing so well. My skin shivered, my nipples hardened, and my heart rate quickened.

Without his coat, Tanner was still huge. He was wearing a different flannel shirt, with a long-sleeved, waffle-patterned undershirt underneath. He was wearing at least two layers of clothes with a winter coat, and I was wearing pajamas and a quilted vest. I did feel a little silly. Luckily, Tanner didn't comment on my attire.

"Thank you," I said. "For the tent and..." I gestured to the coat.

"You're welcome." He didn't smile, but he seemed contented and a little less angry. My eyes roamed over his gorgeous face and down the rest of his body. His forearms were resting on his knees, which were pulled up almost to his chest. He had giant hands. My mind started to wander to places only the mind of a person who hadn't had sex in months and was also sitting in a tent with the god of sex mountain would go.

"You should sit on it."

"Excuse me?" I spluttered. Tanner's voice broke me out of my daydream.

I looked into his face to see him glaring at me. He didn't seem angry, he seemed hungry...for me. I felt my own heart race, and before I could wonder what would happen next. Tanner closed his eyes and turned away from me. After a moment, he regained his composure, and the grumpy mountain man returned.

"The coat. You should sit on it. The ground cover isn't insulated, and those pants don't look warm."

"Oh, right. The coat. Sure. Thanks." I shimmied my butt until I could tuck the bottom of Tanner's coat underneath me, trying to push the image of Tanner's glare out of my mind. He was right again. My ass was apparently going numb from sitting on the ground and tingled as it regained warmth from sitting on the hem of Tanner's coat.

"So," I started to change the subject, "do you plan on making the rounds to your other guests...in preparation for the storm?"

"You're my only guest." A fact he didn't seem altogether happy about.

"Really?" This surprised me. The place was a little outdated, but I was sure he'd found his demographic. This place should always be packed. "I would think this place would always be busy. Do you get a lot of hunters?"

"I don't allow hunters on this land."

"Really, you could make so much money if you just—"

"I said no hunters!" he snapped at me, making me jump. My eyes flicked to the door flap, and he saw, causing his expression to soften to one of concern. "I don't like hunters," he said in a quieter voice.

He put his hand on my knee over his coat. I felt a familiar wave of electricity even through the many layers of fabric and feathers. He felt it too because he was wearing the same momentary expression he wore a moment ago, but more intense. His nostrils flared, and his chest heaved. He looked like he wanted to pounce on me, and I wasn't sure I would have minded. Yes, he was a rude, grumpy asshole, but he was a sexy rude, grumpy asshole, and for some reason, my logic wasn't in control. I was overcome by some primal urge to climb this man like a tree. My heart rate sped up, and the muscles between my thighs clenched.

We stared at each other for what felt like an eternity wrapped up in a second or two. Tanner shut his eyes and drew in a deep breath. He mumbled something that sounded suspiciously like the words, "not mine," but before I could ask him about it, he started speaking again.

"This land has been in my family for generations, and I'm responsible for it. I don't respect people who hunt for sport."

"Okay." I nodded. "No hunters. But that doesn't mean you couldn't turn this place into a decent tourist destination. It has to cost a lot to keep this place up."

"It does, but I'm not good at advertising." One side of his beard twitched in a smile.

Yeah, no shit. And Tanner's interpersonal skills left a lot to be desired. However, he did help me put up my tent and kept me from freezing to death in yoga pants.

"Well, it just so happens that I'm pretty skilled in the marketing department, and I need someone to help me assemble camping equipment. Could you recommend someone?" I smiled at him, and he let out an involuntary chuckle, which must have been painful for him. "You help me navigate the pile of gear in the cabin, and I'll help you spread the word about... Do you have a name for this place?"

"My grandfather called it Black Bear Mountain."

"You really have a thing for bears, don't you?" I was thinking about the internet password and of course, my late-night visitor.

He smiled, but it didn't reach his eyes. "You could say that."

"Okay. Black Bear Mountain Lodges. How does that sound?"

Tanner smiled again. He really liked this idea. This smile was more significant than the last, displaying two rows of gorgeous white teeth. His two front teeth had a small gap. He was grumpy, sexy, but completely adorable, and it made my heart flutter.

"Black Bear Mountain Lodges... I like it."

"Good. Do you have a website?" I asked, having a feeling I already knew the answer. Predictably, he shook his head. "No worries. I happen to know the best graphic designer. You met her yesterday. She can redesign your brochures and build you a website. That's a start."

"And what do you want from me in return for this help?" He fixed his eyes on me with his eyebrows raised.

It took me a few seconds to flip through all of the inappropriate responses that immediately sprang to mind before I could answer him.

"Um, just help me with any of the sponsored products that I can't figure out. Help me take pictures. Stop being a grumpy jerk whenever you see me."

His eyes widened in shock, and he tilted his head.

"What?"

"Yes. You've been condescending and rude every time you've seen me."

"You called me names. Brought three days' worth of snacks to feed yourself for a week, not to mention your 'winter clothes.'" He flicked a glance at my Adidas, which were the only things visible under his massive coat. "Then I bring you food, and I find you working outside, alone in the cold, and half-dressed. I'll be spending most of my time keeping you alive." His grumpy countenance returned.

"I'm sorry to be such a burden," I snapped, pushed his hand off of my knee, and tried to leave the tent. He covered my hand with his, and I froze.

"Chellie." It was the first time he'd said my name, and it flooded my chest with a tingling sensation. "I'm sorry. I didn't mean to offend you. I'm not what you'd call a people person."

I glared at him, but I didn't try to leave the tent again.

"Thank you for your offer, and I don't mind taking care of you."

I tilted my head in confusion. His eyes widened for a second, then he looked away. "Taking care of my guests...at the cabins... I need to leave. Keep the coat. I'll get it later. Put those groceries away."

Then, for the second time, he left without saying goodbye.

5

I'M GOING TO GO KISS A BEAR

There was no storm that night, but my giant furry friend made another appearance at my window. I didn't squeal and run away this time. We just stood on opposite sides of the cabin window staring at each other for a few minutes. I'm not sure how I knew this, but it was definitely the same bear from the previous night.

They were big with glistening black fur and a tan-colored muzzle. Golden brown eyes that glittered in the moonlight surveyed me curiously as I did the same. Their dark coat was shiny. It looked soft, and for an insane moment, I wondered what it would be like to run my fingers through the downy follicles. Then, of course, I reminded myself that I was actually considering petting a bear: a giant, wild, carnivo-rous, big-ass bear.

It was time for me to go to bed.

I checked the locks on the doors and windows. Even though they probably wouldn't do any good if Yogi were really intent on getting in here, for some reason, I knew I didn't have anything to fear. I snuggled into my bed, sent Dawn a text message, letting her know I was still alive, and drifted off to sleep where I dreamed about bears.

———— •••• ————

"So, how's your little project going?" My mother was trying to sound encouraging, and it wasn't her strong suit, so I had to give her an E for effort.

My little project was going well. There was less talk about New Year's Eve, and my numbers were up. Brenda was optimistic, and my sponsors were slowly returning. I was starting to feel in control of my life again.

"Fine," was all I said in response. I really wanted to get off the phone with my mother. I know she didn't call me to talk about my job, because I'm sure she would've called Brenda herself to get the details. She wanted to talk about Mike, his new fiancée, the fact that I wasn't getting any younger and wasn't going to be beautiful forever. The only time she complimented my looks was to remind me how fleeting they were. "Listen, Mother, I need to get an early start styling photos. There's supposed to be a storm, and I want to have enough scheduled in case I lose the internet."

"Oh, Chellie Belly, you have a few minutes to talk to your mother. I wanted to talk to you about the videos you posted on New Year's Eve."

I rolled my eyes. I still hadn't seen them. Brenda had them deleted from my account in about ten minutes. I knew they would live in some dark corner of the internet forever, but they had mostly faded from public consciousness.

"I'd just broken up with my boyfriend and had too much to drink. I'm hardly the only person to make rambling videos about their ex."

"Well, that was awful, and I still can't believe Dawn didn't do anything to help you. I'm talking about the last video. The one with you kissing that stranger."

I knew about this video, again I hadn't seen it.

"Drunk, Mother. I was drunk."

"Well, dear. I just thought that was a phase. I didn't realize you were still having those sorts of inclinations."

"What are you talking about?"

"Oh, Celestine, don't make me say it."

"Say what?" I was genuinely confused. The sensible thing to do would've been to hang up immediately and ask Dawn to send me the video. Instead, I pressed my mother further.

"A woman," she hissed into the phone. "You were kissing a woman." My stomach dropped, and my head started to pound. My mother had a unique form of short-term memory loss that only affected her ability to remember that I was bisexual.

"Are you serious? This is why you're upset?" I usually didn't let my mother bait me like this, but I let my frustration get the best of me.

"Celestine, how do you ever expect to find a decent husband if you behave like this publicly."

"Are you fucking serious?" I shouted. "My boyfriend of a year dumped me and publicly humiliated me, and all you care about is that I made out with a woman—which is not wrong, no matter how many times you try to convince me it is. Have you ever considered that my life doesn't revolve around finding a rich husband before I get crow's feet? I have a career. I have something I'm good at that is solely based on my talent and abilities—"

"And your beauty, Celestine. There are plenty of girls that are more intelligent, more talented, and want what you have but will never get it because they don't have your beauty. I just wish you would understand that and use it to your advantage. All of this internet, social media business is fine, but it's not going to last. You treat me like I'm some kind of villain, but I'm your mother. My job is to look out for your best interests, not to coddle you and your whims."

"My career is not a whim. My sexuality is not a whim."

"Oh, stop being dramatic, Celestine."

I wanted to pick up something big and fragile, so I could throw it across the room and watch it shatter, but that would only serve to prove my mother's point.

"I have to go now. I'm going to go kiss a bear and hope no one films it and uploads it to Snapchat."

"Celestine, you just—"

I didn't hear the rest of her reply. I wanted to throw my phone, but it was too precious. I needed a kickboxing class but didn't think there was an Equinox on this mountain. Instead, I decided to go for a walk, hoping some fresh air could calm me down.

I walked through the woods, stepping over fallen logs and crunching my boots over twigs and leaves, for about fifteen minutes when I heard loud banging noises. My walk slowed, and I saw Tanner standing in front of a large tree stump. He'd picked up a piece of wood with one hand and tossed it on the stump. Then he'd picked up a large ax, raised it, and brought it down with a quick whooshing sound, followed by the loud crack of the log splitting in two.

Tanner, sweating in this cold weather, splitting logs with a giant ax, was the sexiest thing I'd ever seen. This wasn't months of deprivation talking. This was a whole lifetime of thinking I knew what sexy was.

His muscles flexed under his flannel shirt, his face furrowed in concentration, and his chest expanded every time he prepared to bring the ax down. I felt frozen to the spot with slick heat prickling between my legs. Tanner turned to look at me at that moment, and I felt a fleeting moment of embarrassment, wondering if he knew what I was thinking, but that wasn't possible.

"Hi." I stood thirty feet away, behind a bush ogling him like a creep. In my defense, I wasn't aware the hedge was there until Tanner spotted me.

"Need something?" He sounded concerned but not very welcoming. I swallowed a nervous lump and stepped forward.

"I was just out for a walk, and I heard you chopping wood." I took another step closer, and he wore the same curious expression that he wore yesterday in the tent, and it just enhanced my frustration. I didn't know if he wanted to jump me, was terrified of me or was mad at me.

"You're walking around by yourself? You need to be more careful." He said this in a gruff voice and went back to chopping wood. He held the handle of the ax higher and swung it with such force the log not only split in two, but the pieces went flying off the stump. He was pissed, and it started to piss me off a little. I still carried more than a little pent-up rage from my phone call, and I was tired of people treating me like I was some delicate little flower. My mother pressured me to use my beauty to trap a wealthy man, and Tanner wanted me to stay locked up in the cabin like Rapunzel.

"You know I'm not as weak and clueless as you think I am." I marched up to him and reached down to pick up a log. Tanner had been grabbing these things with one hand and tossing them on the stump like they were balloons. My clumsy endeavor involved crouching down and clutching a log with both hands, stumbling over to the stump, and dumping it on top. He watched the spectacle with a bemused expression, not bothering to try to assist me. Once I had the log positioned upright in the middle of the stump, heaving, and sweating, I held out my arm for the ax.

"No," Tanner said. He was trying to keep a straight face, but his beard and mustache twitched.

"Give me the ax," I demanded.

"Chellie, this ax is too big and too heavy. You'd chop off one of your legs trying to swing it."

His words hurt me. He was probably right, but hearing another person tell me that I wasn't capable of doing something was too much to take. Though I tried to fight them, my eyes stung with tears. My eyelids opened and closed furiously, trying to keep the tears from falling, and I turned away from Tanner. I'd taken two steps in the direction of my cabin when he called to me in a softer tone.

"Hey, Chellie, I'm sorry. Wait."

I turned around, and Tanner was holding a smaller ax. Compared to the one he was using to split logs, this one looked like a child's toy.

"Try this one." He'd even managed a small smile.

"Really?" I sniffled and walked closer. He nodded and handed me the ax. The ax felt huge and heavy in my hands, and now I felt foolish, wondering if I'd even be able to pick up the one Tanner was using.

"Know what to do?" he asked. I shook my head.

Tanner walked up until he was directly behind me. His fingers wrapped around my shoulders and gently positioned them. His touch sent little jolts of electricity through my body. Tanner's fingertips skated down my body, gently adjusting my posture, like a yoga instructor. He squared my hips and guided my legs into a grounded stance. His palms glided down my biceps and forearms until his large, calloused and surprisingly warm hands covered mine on the handle of the ax.

"Put one hand under the head, like this." He guided my fist up the shaft, I mean, handle of the ax until I was resting directly under the cold, metal head. "Good," his voice came in a strained whisper. The sexual tension formed a cloud that could've strangled us. Tanner pressed our bodies closer, and let's just say, my wood-chopping instructor added another log to the fire.

"Okay, as you swing, you're going to guide the blade of the ax directly to your target by bringing your fists together like this." With his hands still covering mine, he guided my fists down the shaft—dammit— the handle of the ax until our hands met at the base of the...handle. Then he brought my fists up again and down again. This was too much. I could feel my body, some parts more than others, prickling with heat even though it was freezing outside.

"Okay." He stepped back, causing my body to be enveloped in an icy chill that made me shiver. "Want to try it on your own?"

No. I'd have liked to continue pumping my fists up and down the shaft of Tanner's ax while still enveloped in the warmth of the waves of heat emanating from his body.

"Um, sure. I'll give it a try." I gave him a small smile, which he returned.

"Okay." He placed a smaller log on the stump and centered it. "Aim for the outer edge of the log. Avoid knots, and if you can find a crack to hit, it will make your job a lot easier."

I nodded, narrowed my focus, and stared at the log. There was a large crack running down two-thirds, and I pictured my mother's face right in the middle. I squared my shoulders, brought the ax up the way Tanner showed me, and brought it down with as much power as I could. The blade of the ax hit the crack dead center, and the log split in two, with the halves rolling off of the stump. I grinned triumphantly at Tanner, who looked genuinely surprised, which only made me smile harder.

My ax swing was so forceful that the blade of the ax got stuck in the stump. I wiggled it to get it unstuck, and when it came free, I was unprepared and stumbled backward into Tanner, who also wasn't prepared but managed to catch me and the ax before we tumbled onto the cold ground.

"Sorry." I laughed breathlessly as I lay on top of his chest where I landed. He was flat on his back with the ax held in his outstretched hand, looking at me with an odd expression. It was a mixture of amusement, wonder, and longing. He definitely wasn't annoyed, and it made my chest flood with a warmth that wasn't arousal...it wasn't all arousal. Our gaze met, and something in Tanner's eyes was so familiar, but I couldn't put my finger on it. It made me feel safe and cared for, and for reasons I couldn't explain, I leaned down and pressed our lips together.

Tanner let out a small noise that sounded like a growl, and I swear, every muscle between my thighs contracted. His giant hands wrapped around my waist, his fingers found the hem of my shirt, and I soon felt his rough fingertips ghosting along the bare skin of my lower back. My legs spread, and I straddled him, pressing myself against his erection desperate for the pressure and friction. I pushed my hands under his wool cap, pushing it off of his head so I could tangle my fingers in his hair.

Tanner's tongue was licking at the seam of my lips, begging for entrance, and I gave it to him. Our kiss was a furious tangle of lips, tongue, and teeth. Our bodies were a tangle of arms, legs, and winter clothes. I was so turned on, I'd forgotten it was winter. My skin was flushed with heat as I continued to press myself into my sexy lumberjack. If Tanner wanted to tear off my clothes and fuck me on the hard ground outside of his cabin, I would let him and beg him for more. Our embrace continued to ramp up in heat and intensity.

Tanner moved on to kissing my cheek and nibbling on my ear. He ghosted tiny pecks and licks on my neck until I felt his facial hair tickling the spot where my neck and shoulder met. An involuntary moan escaped my lips right before Tanner pulled away the collar of my sweater and dug his teeth into my shoulder, breaking the skin.

"Ow!" I squealed and pushed away from him. "What was that?" It definitely hurt, but I wasn't as upset as I thought I should've been. Strangely, I kind of liked it. No, I loved it. The sensation sent a jolt of electricity through my body, good electricity, that settled between my legs causing my core to throb.

The bite was more of a shock than anything else. I wasn't exactly a stranger to over-exuberant sex, but I would've appreciated a little warning. When I looked down at Tanner, his eyes were wide with an expression that looked like fear.

"Fuck, Chellie. I'm sorry. I shouldn't have done that."

"It's okay, Tanner. I kind of liked it. I just didn't think you were into that kind of stuff, but I guess you never know, right?" I giggled, and Tanner's panic-stricken expression never faltered.

"You don't understand. I fucked up." He sat up and gently lifted me off of his lap like I was a rag doll and set me down on the ground beside him. "I shouldn't have marked you."

"Marked me?" I laughed. "If you're afraid of your bite leaving a scar, I have a cream that would take care of that. Do you have some kind of contagious illness I should be concerned about?" I laughed again, hoping I'd made a joke.

"No, I would never put you in danger like that." He'd pulled his knees up to his chest, rested his elbows on his legs, and put his head in his hands.

"Am I that bad a kisser?" I tried to make another joke. I was desperate not to feel the sting of rejection again, but Tanner still didn't break.

"You're an amazing kisser, but I'm sorry. This can't happen." He pushed himself to his feet and reached down to help me stand. I slapped his hand away and scrambled to my feet, my face burning with anger and embarrassment. "Chellie, please, I can't stand to see you upset."

"You should have thought about that before you 'marked me'"—I made air quotes as I backed away from him—"or whatever the hell just happened here." I spat the words out between sobs and took off running towards my cabin.

6

GET YOUR ASS UP AND HELP ME

I shut myself in the cabin and let my tears fall. Of all of the shitty things that have happened to me this year—which consisted of three weeks so far—Tanner treating me like an actual piece of meat and then throwing me away was the worst.

He came to my cabin after I'd locked myself in, and I sent him away. He refused to leave and then finally relented if I promised to use the first aid kit he'd left on the porch. When I opened the door to retrieve it, he was pacing in front of the cabin nervously, and it made me feel the tiniest iota of sympathy, which I quickly doused.

I cleaned, disinfected, and bandaged the bite. I flopped on the bed and checked my scheduled posts to make sure they were running. I checked my comments, did the requisite number of likes and replies before turning my phone off and crying myself to sleep.

I woke up in the middle of the night and went to the kitchen for a glass of water. I walked past the window, and as I suspected, my bear friend was curled up on the ground. Its head perked up when it saw me, and it ventured closer to the window, closer than usual.

The golden-brown eyes that usually surveyed me were sad instead of curious, but maybe I was projecting because I was also sad instead of curious. Unexpected tears rolled down my cheeks again.

I felt lost and alone. The only two people in the world who cared about me were over four hours away, and I looked to a bear for solace. After briefly considering scheduling a few more weeks of posts and sneaking back to the city and away from Tanner, I dismissed the idea and went to bed.

My host was at my door again early the next morning. He wore the same clothes he had on the day before, with dark circles under his eyes. I wondered if he'd gotten any sleep last night. Then I tried to convince myself that I didn't care. I told him I didn't want to talk to him, but he wouldn't go away until I let him stock the extra firewood he'd spent the morning chopping. He asked me how the bite was healing and I told him it was fine, not exchanging another word with him.

The curious thing about the bite is that it wasn't healing. It was healed. When I woke up the morning after our ill-fated tumble in the woods and removed the bandage, the bite was completely healed. Tanner's teeth marks were still there, but they were faint golden-brown imprints. It didn't even hurt. I started rubbing the scar prevention cream on them, but something told me it was too late. Tanner had, in fact, marked me. I wanted to talk to him about it, but I was still too angry, and the marks were so faint that they were barely noticeable.

Three days had passed since our kiss. I spent the time focused on posting about things I could use in the cabin because I was avoiding Tanner. I also didn't tell Dawn about the kiss. He showed up again in the morning with another excuse to check on me, and I was frustrated with his strange behavior. I didn't feel unsafe or like Tanner was stalking me.

On the contrary, it made me feel safe. Tanner wasn't aggressive and didn't cross any boundaries. He seemed genuinely concerned for me, and it confused the hell out of me. He doesn't want me. Then he does. Then he doesn't, but won't leave me alone?

THAT NIGHT when I woke up, I went to the window and my bear—yes, I called it my bear—wasn't at the window. Feeling even more lonely and pathetic because I'd spent the day looking forward to staring at a bear, I decided to call Dawn and talk to a person.

I still hadn't told her about my encounter with Tanner because I was still hurt and embarrassed, but she was my best friend, and keeping it to myself for three days hadn't won me any medals. I was making bear dates, for God's sake, a clear sign that I'd gone insane.

I tried to dial her, but I couldn't get a signal. I walked around the cabin, holding the phone near every window. I wondered if this was because of the coming storm Tanner talked about or, maybe, the universe was conspiring to make me as miserable as possible.

One bar. The reception was still terrible.

I opened the front door. Two bars.

I stepped onto the porch. A flicker between two and three bars.

I went back inside and quickly dressed. Adequately outfitted in enough layers of wool and quilted attire to make Tanner proud, if I cared about Tanner's opinion—which I didn't—I ventured outside, holding my phone over my head. The flicker of the third bar got stronger the further I got from the cabin.

I let out a little squeal of delight when I saw the fourth bar flicker. I dialed Dawn. The phone rang three times before her voicemail picked up.

"Hello. This is Dawn. Leave a message after the beep or better yet, send me a text because it's 2019, not 1994." There was a beep. I took a deep breath.

"Hey, Dawn, it's Chellie. I wish you would've picked up because I really need to talk to you. Something happened between Tanner and me, and I'm going a little crazy. I shouldn't be leaving this in a voicemail, but—" I paused. I heard a noise. It sounded like the crack of branches. There was nothing when I looked in the direction of the noise, and I also noticed that my cabin wasn't visible.

Shit.

"Why were you walking around by yourself? You should be more careful."

The memory of Tanner's admonishing voice echoed, and for once, I wish I'd listened to him.

"—Dawn, I have to call you back," I whispered, feeling silly as soon as I ended the call. The woods were eerily quiet, and I started to wonder if I'd imagined the noise. Then I saw it.

A large golden-brown cat stalked across the path. Yellowish-green eyes caught the moonlight and glowed. My body froze, but I forced myself to take three long deep breaths. Now, I really wished I was on the phone with Dawn. She would have some priceless piece of trivia picked up from the hours of the nature shows she watches that would tell me exactly how to deal with a mountain lion attack. She spouted information about the Catskill Mountains the whole way up here. Did she say anything about mountain lions? Yes, she said they'd gone extinct in the 1800s. Well, someone didn't send Simba the memo.

The lion stopped in front of me at a distance I estimated at thirty or forty feet, definitely not enough of a head start to get to my cabin. I probably couldn't outrun it. I didn't see any sticks or rocks I could hit it with. I could try running in a zig-zag pattern. *No, Chellie, that's alligators.* Was I supposed to punch it in the nose? *No, that's sharks.* I couldn't think of anything that was going to save me. So, I just continued staring at the lion. I thought about Tanner. He'd know what to do, but for once he wasn't hovering around.

Resigned to my fate, I decided that I would crouch into a ball and protect my face as much as I could, but my body was still frozen. I couldn't believe this was how I was going to die; not parasailing in Belize or cliff diving in Jamaica. I was going to get eaten by a freaking mountain lion in the Catskill Mountains. Hot tears ran down my face, and I watched the cat crouch and bounce its back legs preparing to pounce. It leaped forward, and my muscles finally reacted. A scream left my body, and my muscles released, allowing me to crumple in a ball on the forest floor and squeeze my eyes shut.

I waited to be mauled, but nothing happened. My eyes jerked open when I heard the snarling of the cat and something else, something more primal and deeper. It was the roar of a bear, my bear. The bear and the mountain lion were embroiled in a fight, and I was a spectator. A few stunned seconds went by before my bear turned and looked directly at me. Its face was full of anger and fury. I realized I was outside in the dark with two ferocious, carnivorous wild animals without the four walls of the cabin to protect me. I had to get the fuck out of here. I had to try.

I slowly rose to my feet, maintaining eye contact with the bear. It let out a loud growl that seemed to be directed at me that shook me to my core. I started to back away as it stared. While the bear was fixated on me, the mountain lion jumped on its back and sunk its teeth into its black fur, causing the bear to rear up on its back legs growling. With them both distracted, I took the opportunity to turn and haul ass towards Tanner's cabin. Mine was too far away, and I'd take a million *I told you so*s and derisive sneers if it meant not getting eaten by a bear and lion.

Running as fast as I could and not daring to look back, I leaped over the stairs onto Tanner's porch and started banging on the front door. There was no answer making my heart race even faster. I screamed Tanner's name and started kicking the door. No response came making my tears come more furiously. The ax he taught me to chop wood with was still lying near the stump, so I grabbed it and returned to the porch to wait for him to come home.

AFTER WHAT SEEMED LIKE HOURS—WITH no sign of the bear or lion—but what my watch told me was twenty minutes, I saw a giant figure limping towards Tanner's cabin.

It was Tanner, and he was hurt, bleeding. He made it to the porch and collapsed against the stairs. He was barefoot, in jeans and just one flannel shirt that was soaked with blood. He must've been attacked by the mountain lion. Or the bear. Or both.

"Tanner," I screamed. He was barely conscious, but we had to get in the cabin before he passed out. There was no way I could get him inside by myself.

"Tanner." I slapped his face. "You have to help me. We have to get you inside."

He looked up at me. His face flooded with an expression that looked like relief, but I could tell he was a lot of pain.

"You're okay," he whispered.

"Yes," I hissed, "but you're not. We have to get inside right now. Please. Just a few feet."

"You're okay," he whispered again.

"Yes, I'm fine, but I won't be unless we get inside. Get your ass up and help me."

Tanner got to his feet. With me to guide him, we made it into his cabin and into his room.

Tanner's cabin was bigger than mine with huge everything. All the furniture was Tanner-sized. It looked antique, and hand-carved. I wasn't surprised to see a lot of bears chiseled into the furniture and moldings.

I managed to help him to bed and out of his blood-soaked shirt. His jeans were also covered in blood, but when I went to pull them off, I quickly discovered that he wasn't wearing anything underneath them. If that wasn't strange enough, Tanner's injuries were deep cuts and scratches, but his clothes were undisturbed. Yes, they were soaked in blood, but it was as if he was naked when he was attacked, then got dressed after.

This was crazy. I had to be suffering from some adrenaline-induced psychosis. Tending to Tanner's injuries was the most important thing. I needed to focus on that.

There was a first aid kit in his bathroom. I cleaned and bandaged the cuts on his back and shoulder as best I could. Some of them looked like bites, and some looked like scratches. I guessed that they came from the mountain lion. If they were from the bear, they would've been bigger.

I peeled Tanner's jeans off and tended to the injuries there while trying to distract myself from the fact that Tanner was huge everywhere. I managed to change his sheets by rolling him from one end of the bed to the other. There was some stew in the fridge, so I reheated it and managed to get him to eat some of it and drink some water. I also started a fire. By the time I was finished, I was physically exhausted.

Tending to Tanner pulled my focus away from the fact that I almost died tonight, and once I was done, the realization set in. My body started to shake of its own volition, and my chest heaved with sobs. Tanner called me over to him, and when I was close enough to touch, he captured my arm and pulled me into bed with him, carefully tucking me into the crook of his arm, to avoid his injuries, where I continued to sob until I fell asleep.

7

HONEY? HOW VERY ON-BRAND

W hen I woke several hours later, it was still dark outside, and Tanner was still asleep. I was enveloped in the warmth of his massive body, inhaling his earthy, sweaty scent. His arm was heavy, and with a little resistance, I managed to move it off of my body and sit up. My head was throbbing from crying so hard. I could also feel the puffiness and irritation of my skin and wished I had my makeup bag, though not enough to fight a mountain lion and bear to go get it, but close. The fire had gone out, so I restarted it, refilled the pitcher of water by the bed, and opened the first aid kit preparing to clean and re-bandage Tanner's scratches and bites.

He barely stirred as I slowly peeled the medical tape off of his shoulder. I lifted the bandage, and what I saw made me jump. I leaped backward off the bed and away from Tanner so fast that the first aid kit dropped to the floor, scattering supplies everywhere.

Tanner jumped awake at the noise, calling my name. His eyes focused on me, and my face must have displayed the horror and confusion I felt.

"What's wrong?" He held his arms out to me, beckoning me to come back to bed, but I only took a step further away.

I opened my mouth to speak, but no words came out, so I pointed to his shoulder. He ripped the bandage the rest of the way off, saw what I'd seen, and deflated.

The deep, angry bites, cuts, and scratches that were fresh and oozing blood a few hours ago were gone. Unlike my miraculously healed bite, there was no trace. It was like they never existed except for the pile of bloody sheets, clothes, and bandages.

"Chellie, I can explain."

"What the fuck?" I said when I could finally speak. I tugged at the collar of my shirt to show Tanner the pale golden remnants of the bite mark he gave me on my shoulder. "What the fuck is going on?"

"Please calm down. It's going to be okay. You're safe. I promise." His deep, soothing voice did have a calming effect, but something strange was going on here. My instincts told me to run, but I couldn't because there was a bear and a mountain lion prowling the woods.

Tanner got out of bed to approach me, momentarily forgetting he was naked. My eyes instinctively traveled south, and he grabbed a sheet and wrapped it around his waist.

"Hold on." He went to a large dresser and dressed in a pair of boxer briefs and a t-shirt after pulling off the rest of my bandages, revealing more unblemished skin. He held his hand out to me, and after a few seconds of deliberation, I accepted it. We walked into the living room, where he deposited me on the couch and wrapped me in a quilt.

He went to the kitchen for a few minutes, leaving me alone in the living room, trying not to panic. My hands began to tremble, so I folded them in my lap. I was seriously formulating an escape plan that involved me running through the woods dragging a giant ax. Then Tanner returned with a steaming bowl of stew and a giant mug of something that was also steaming.

"I'm not hungry," I mumbled right before my stomach gave a traitorous growl. I couldn't remember the last time I ate. I didn't think I was hungry, but my body didn't agree. I took the bowl from Tanner's hand and set it on my lap. He watched me take a spoonful, and he visibly relaxed. Fuck, that stew was tasty. It was beefy and fatty with the right ratio of broth and root vegetables. I bet if Tanner gave me the recipe, I could post a video of —*dammit, Chellie*. Not now. I needed to turn my business brain off and focus.

Once I'd eaten enough to satisfy the food police, he handed me the mug.

"What is this?" I looked at him skeptically.

"It's tea." He actually had the nerve to smirk at me. "Chellie, I don't know how many times you need me to say this, but I'll say it as many times as it takes to convince you. I would never do anything to hurt you."

I sighed and took the tea, brought the mug to my lips and sipped. It was delicious with a little bite.

"What's in this?" I licked my lips, a gesture that didn't go unnoticed.

"Tea, lemon, brandy, and honey."

"Honey? How very on-brand." I indicated all of the wood carved bears around the cabin.

He responded with a chuckle that didn't quite reach his eyes.

"Are you gonna tell me what's going on?"

He heaved a deep sigh and lowered himself to the floor at my feet.

"I've never talked about this before, and I'm not good at conversation, but know that everything I'm telling you is true, and you have nothing to fear from me." He clasped the hand that wasn't holding my mug.

Tanner was right. He was terrible at conversation because now I was more afraid than ever. Still, I wanted him to tell me whatever he needed to say to me, so I took a deep breath, hoping to bring my heart rate under control and nodded.

"Chellie, you ever heard of a shifter?"

I snatched my hand away.

"Yes, I know what shifters are, and I also know that shifters aren't real."

His eyes widened in shock.

"How?"

"My nana used to tell me about shifters. I thought she made them up. Are you telling me that shifters are real? Are you a shifter?"

He nodded.

"Are you nodding because shifters are real or because you are a shifter?" I really needed him to be completely clear because my heart was thudding in my ears, and nothing felt true.

"Both."

I took a long draught from my mug and shook my head.

"No."

"It's true."

"No. This is some kind of crazy hallucination. I'm dreaming. I'm asleep."

"Chellie, you're not dreaming. I can show you."

"Show me? Do you mean you're going to turn into an animal in front of me?"

"If you want. I think it might be the fastest way to convince you."

"Okay," I whispered and took another long sip from the mug to calm my nerves.

Tanner left the room and came back with a legal pad and black marker. He scribbled in the book, tearing sheets off, making a small pile. When he was done writing, he began moving the furniture in the living room, including the couch I was on, clearing an ample space. My head was spinning. Was Tanner actually gonna transform in front of me? How would I react? What the hell was in this tea? His voice broke my chain of thought.

"Do you want to see me change, or I can go to the bedroom?"

"I think I should see you."

"Don't be afraid."

"Okay," I lied.

Tanner arranged the yellow sheets of paper on the floor at his feet. At first, I strained to see what the sheets of paper said, but Tanner drew my focus when he took a few steps back and turned away from me. His t-shirt and boxers fell to the floor in a small pile. His muscles began to flex and contract, then right before my eyes, he...shifted. His arms and legs shortened.

My heart raced. Tanner's chest and torso expanded.

Oh my God. This was really happening.

He was changing. His entire body sprouted fur, and when he turned to face me, I recognized him immediately.

It was my bear. The creature that had come to my window every night for the past week was Tanner. I thought back to our kiss and realized why his eyes felt so familiar. Tanner was my bear.

I sat frozen on the couch, but not in fear. Shock and confusion paralyzed me. The wheels in my head were turning, and I was putting the pieces together.

The bear walked forward and tapped its muzzle on one of the sheets of paper. I leaned over to read it.

You okay?

I looked up at the bear that was Tanner. He was still in there, and he was communicating. I thought back to all of the nights he sat outside my window. It was him watching over me.

"I'll be spending most of my time keeping you alive." He meant the words literally.

"Yes. Can you understand me?"

He tapped his nose on another sheet.

Yes.

"You saved me from the mountain lion?"

Yes.

I swallowed a lump in my throat. I didn't want to think about where I would be if Tanner, in his bear form, hadn't shown up when he did. I also remembered the mountain lion sinking its teeth into Tanner's shoulder, allowing me to escape.

"Thank you." It was all I could say.

The bear let out an impatient huff. Yup, it was definitely Tanner, and I think I just witnessed the bear equivalent of *I told you so.*

"Is it safe to touch you?"

Yes.

I walked forward, and Tanner lowered his head. I ran my fingers through the downy fur on his neck, and he angled his head, guiding my hand to a spot behind his ear. When I found it and began to scratch, he let out a low satisfied growl and closed his eyes. It was strange how right it felt to comfort him this way. I could spend the rest of my life tangling my fingers in his fur while he purred like a cat.

After a few minutes, I stepped back to see him again. He ultimately lowered himself to the floor and gazed at me. I looked at all of the sheets of paper on the floor before I picked one and held it up for him to see.

Want me to change back?

He stood on all fours and shuddered, turning into the human Tanner again. He quickly dressed and sat on the floor in the middle of the room, eyeing me and waiting for me to speak.

A few long minutes passed before I took the quilt off of the couch and sat next to Tanner on the floor, draping the quilt over our shoulders. I handed him the mug, and he took a sip before handing it back to me. We stared into the fireplace.

"Was the mountain lion a shifter too?"

"Nope. That was a mountain lion."

"I thought that mountain lions were extinct in the Catskill Mountains."

"Extinct doesn't mean there are none left. It means there are very few. And no hunters make it easier for species to thrive."

"Why weren't you at my window tonight?"

"The mountain lion was close, and I was trying to keep it away from your cabin."

"Why didn't you warn me?"

"I told you not to go walking around by yourself."

"Oh yeah." I nodded and took another sip of tea.

"Yeah," he muttered.

I leaned my head on his shoulder, and he put his arm around my waist. I sighed in contentment, and Tanner dropped a kiss on the top of my head as we continued to stare into the crackling fire.

This entire night was batshit crazy. I was almost killed by a mountain lion, saved by a bear, and the bear turned out to be Tanner. All those years of bedtime stories my grandmother told me about shifters were true. Tanner had transformed before my eyes, and now I was cuddling under a quilt with him. The most insane thing is that it felt right. Here in this cabin, together and safe with all of our truths laid bare—that was unintentional—was the only place in the world I wanted to be.

"Chellie," Tanner called my name softly, and I turned to look up at him.

"Yeah?"

"You're not weak and clueless."

"Sure." I rolled my eyes and chuckled.

"I mean, I thought so at first, but I was wrong. You're clever, intelligent, resourceful, strong, courageous..."

I gazed up at him in disbelief, tears welled in my eyes.

"What's wrong?" he asked.

"Nothing." I sniffled. "Keep saying nice things about me."

One side of his mouth twitched, and his arm tightened around my waist and pulled me closer.

"And you're funny. I've waited my whole life to feel this way about someone, and when you showed up, you weren't what I was expecting."

"Tanner, what are you talking about?"

"Did your nana tell you about fated mates?"

"Yes." I nodded. "Fated mates are two people—sometimes more than two—that are destined to be together. When they find each other, it's an instant connection that can never be broken."

He nodded, still gazing at me.

"What? Do you think we're fated mates?"

"I know we are." His voice seemed more resigned than excited.

"How do you know?"

"I smelled it when I first went to your cabin. Then when I saw you, I knew."

I remember when we locked eyes the first moment we met. There was definitely a moment where I felt something magical and tangible between us, but it was quickly extinguished by Tanner's grumpy attitude.

"I thought you hated me."

"I hated that I could never hate you."

"Wow. You really know how to sweep a girl off of her feet." I pushed his hand off of my waist and tucked a lock of hair behind my ear. Tanner scooped me up and deposited me in his lap.

"I'm more literal than literary, Chellie." He laughed. OMG, Tanner just made a joke. I grinned at him. "When my grandfather told me about my mate, I was expecting someone that I'd have more in common with, and well, we couldn't be more different. But he also said my mate would be fierce, loyal, tenacious, and protective. You're all of those things, and I was too busy fighting the inevitable to see them."

"You know that I was with Mike for almost a year."

"I know." He held me tighter.

"Isn't there like a bro code or something? Like you can't date your friend's ex."

He laughed. "No. But even if there was, fate overrides the bro code."

"Does Mike know...about you?"

"If he does, he's never said anything. Growing up, everyone just thought my parents were strict. I couldn't go to sleepovers, play sports, or hang out on weekends."

He shrugged and gave me a sad smile. I wrapped my arms around his neck and squeezed. I imagined him sitting on the side while Mike and his other friends played hockey on the pond behind Mike's house. Tanner planted a kiss on my forehead.

"What if I was married when we met?"

"Fate," he replied.

"What if I was in love with someone else?"

"Ever been in love with anyone else?"

I didn't need to think long before I shook my head. Mike's breakup stung hard because it was public and unexpected, but when I thought about it, I was never in love with Mike, not really. We liked the same things and had fun together, but we never had a deep connection like the one I felt for the man who held me in his arms. Mike had also never fought a mountain lion for me, so Tanner had that going for him.

"So, is that what this bite is?" I tugged at the collar of my shirt to expose the skin on my shoulder. Tanner lightly ghosted his fingertips over the teeth marks before gently pressing a kiss to them. "You marked me, and now I belong to you."

"Chellie, you're my mate. That bite mark is me pledging my life, my heart, and my soul to you. I will provide for you, care for you, and protect you as long as there's breath in my body. That bite mark means I belong to you."

8

BEST INSTAGRAM BOYFRIEND EVER

Tanner's declaration ignited something in me. I turned in Tanner's lap and straddled him, wrapping my arms around his neck again and pressed our faces together. He let out a low growl, as he did during our first kiss, and clutched me around the waist, forced his tongue in my mouth, probing and exploring while his hands did the same to my body, leaving trails of heat over the skin he could reach under my layers of clothes.

Tanner was rock hard, and his thin boxers left nothing to the imagination. He rolled me onto my back and pressed himself between my legs, where I was throbbing with arousal, eliciting involuntary whimpers from me.

"Tanner, I need you," I moaned. "Right now."

He began to peel off my layers of clothes, his impatience growing with each reveal of another garment.

"You picked tonight to listen to me about dressing properly," he grumbled. I laughed and bicycled my legs to assist him as he yanked off the last layer, a pair of wool tights along with my panties.

Tanner took in the sight of my bare legs and inhaled deeply. I suddenly got self-conscious.

"I was wearing all these layers of clothes and running through the woods... I can hop in the shower really quick if you want... Tanner, say something."

"You smell delicious." He leaned forward and planted a kiss on my bare thigh, making me shiver. "Can I taste you?"

"Are you going to bite me again?"

"No... Unless you want me to?" He smirked.

"Then, by all means..." I separated my knees and displayed myself for him. His eyes flashed and darkened as he leaned forward. My eyelids fluttered closed as I felt the warm tickle of his breath against my sex, followed by the warm, slick pass of his tongue. He parted my labia, pressing his tongue into my core, gently sucking and tasting me as I writhed in pleasure.

"Oh, Tanner. It feels so good. You feel so good."

The fingertips of his large hands pressed into my thighs, prying them apart, opening me further for him.

The tip of his tongue licked at my inner labia, gently grazing but not touching the sensitive bundle of nerves where I needed to feel him. I wiggled and squirmed, trying to get myself into a better position.

"Soon, beautiful." He smiled up at me before planting a kiss on my thigh. He was torturing me on purpose.

"Dammit, Tanner," I whined. "I need to come. Please, you're killing me."

He grinned at me again. "You taste so good like this. So open and greedy for me." He pressed a kiss between my legs directly on my clit, making me jump, but still not enough for a release.

"Oh my God," I moaned. Just as I contemplated grabbing fistfuls of his hair and grinding myself into his face, he slipped one of his giant fingers into my crevice and massaged me from the inside.

Well, shit.

My body went still, and my chest began to heave. I felt like I was floating. Tanner's tongue resumed its exploration between my legs, and I felt him slide another finger into me. My body greedily accepted his invading digits, and my muscles pulsed around them. My hips began to move of their own volition, and I'd made a noise I'd never made before.

"Ready?" he asked me. I was beyond ready, but I couldn't make my voice work to answer him, so I nodded instead. He covered my clit with his lips and sucked lightly, and within seconds I'd crested. Every muscle in my body tensed before my hips jerked and spasmed. I moaned Tanner's name before floating back to Earth with the occasional body spasm. Tanner gently caressed me as the tide of my orgasm ebbed.

He planted a kiss on my bare thighs.

"You okay?" he asked, with a grin on his face. I managed a weak smile and nodded again.

If I didn't believe in fated mates before, I definitely did now. I would fight a mountain lion for the orgasm Tanner just gave me. My entire body was limp and an endorphin-heavy euphoria washed over me. Tanner gently peeled me out of the rest of my clothes, and I was barely able to help. He undressed and wrapped us in the quilt where we stared into the fire while he stroked my back.

———— •••• ————

I WANTED to make love that night, but Tanner wanted to wait.

"Chellie, this is a lot of information to take in. I don't want to overwhelm you." He molded his body around mine and kissed my shoulder.

"I think we moved past overwhelming Chellie with that orgasm." I tucked my toes between his calves, and his chest vibrated with laughter against my back. "Where did you learn to do that?"

"You really want to know?" He was grazing his fingertips over the curve of my hips with his lips still pressed to my shoulder.

"No, not really." I grinned and flipped over to face him. "So, what exactly are we waiting for?"

"Chellie, I don't have any condoms."

"It's okay, Tanner. I'm on the pill, and you could pull out."

"I couldn't take that risk. A life with me would be different than what you're used to. I want you to understand what you're getting into."

"But aren't we fated mates. We don't have a choice, right?" I smiled up at him, but he didn't return my smile. He stared into the fire.

"Of course, you have a choice. We're soul mates, but that doesn't mean you have to stay with me."

"Don't you want me to stay with you?" My stomach started to knot.

He refocused and looked at me. "Yes. I want you to stay with me. I never want to let you out of my sight, but your life is different than mine. I wouldn't care about you if I expected you to give up what makes you happy. Part of being your mate is making you happy. Could you see yourself living in the mountains for the rest of your life?"

I didn't answer him right away, because I wasn't sure. Something deep inside me told me that I belonged wherever Tanner was, but did that mean that I had to give up my career?

"You could live in the city with me."

"Chellie, I need to protect this land, and I can't go for long periods without shifting."

"But you went to school with Mike. I know Wappingers Falls isn't the big city, but surely you weren't shifting every night?"

"My mother would send me to stay with my grandfather every weekend, and I would shift with him. But weekdays were excruciating for me. My mom and my stepdad did their best, but I know raising me wasn't easy."

"Your mom isn't a shifter?"

"No, she's human, like you." He kissed my shoulder again. "She met, fell in love, married my dad, and had me. We lived here with my grandparents, and we were happy. Then, when I was five, my dad died." He paused, and I put my hand over his and squeezed. "My mom remarried and moved with my stepfather to Dutchess County."

"How did your father die?" I immediately regretted the question. I didn't want to force him to dredge up painful memories, but Tanner didn't hesitate to answer me.

"My dad and I were foraging in the woods as bears, and he was shot by a hunter. He was protecting me."

"I'm so sorry." I felt my eyes stinging with tears. Tanner looked down into my face and wiped away my tears with his thumb before kissing me. "That's why you don't allow hunters on the land."

He nodded.

"Chellie, I want you to be sure I'm what you want. It's not something you can decide in one night. When my mom lost my dad, she had my grandparents to help her. If we had a child and something happened to me, you would be raising a bear shifter by yourself."

"Whoa. Don't you think it's a little early to talk about kids."

"Not if we're serious. Any child we have would be a shifter."

I went silent. I wasn't sure I even wanted kids until this moment. My mind suddenly flooded with images of Tanner tossing a toddler in the air, teaching a little girl how to split logs, and I saw little black bear cubs with tan muzzles playing in a pile of leaves.

"You're right, Tanner. This is a lot to take in. I feel like I want this. I want you and a life with you, but you're right. This isn't a decision I should take lightly."

"Good." He snaked his arm around my waist and pulled me into him, kissing me again.

"Are you sure we shouldn't have sex? I think it could really aid in my decision-making process."

Tanner belly-laughed and I loved seeing his smile with his tiny gap in his front teeth.

"How about the next best thing?" He began kissing a trail down my body until he swirled his tongue around my navel, making me shudder.

"Okay. If you insist." I sighed as I felt his palm slide between my thighs. "But only if you let me return the favor."

Tanner answered me with a growl right before he did something with his tongue that made my back arch, and my eyes roll to the back of my head.

———— • • • • ————

"Best Instagram boyfriend ever." I laughed as I scrolled through my photos and videos. Tanner was a quick study. We had spent the last hour splitting firewood and making videos.

"Thank you." He leaned down and kissed me. "You're the best marketing manager I've ever had."

"I'm the only marketing manager you've ever had." It's been two weeks since the mountain lion incident, and Tanner and I have been getting closer than ever. We kept our business arrangement going. As promised, he helped me assemble camping equipment and shoot photos and videos, but he took it a step further and helped me come up with new ideas for posts like identifying poisonous plants and hiking tips. We even made a video together, cooking his delicious stew. I learned it was his grandmother's recipe.

When we weren't working, we spent a lot of time cuddling, kissing, talking, and doing everything except having sex.

If I wanted to go hiking, sometimes Tanner would accompany me as a bear, and I was surprised at how natural it felt.

The winter storm we were promised finally hit. We'd stockpiled enough food and firewood. Tanner had everything we needed to be comfortable, and when the electricity and the internet went out for three days, I barely noticed.

⸻ • • • • ⸻

ONCE I FOUND a perfect wood-chopping video to post to my stories, I turned to begin stomping through the snow back to Tanner's cabin. I'd made it two steps before my mountain man scooped me in his arms, kissed me, and carried me towards the house. My phone rang when he set me down on the porch. I ignored it.

"Want to get that?"

"No." It was from Brenda. I usually didn't ignore her calls, but I'd been scheduling posts, checking to make sure that they posted, and they seemed to be doing well, but my heart wasn't in it. My focus has shifted—no pun intended—and though I was doing my job, it suddenly didn't seem that important. The thrill I used to get from watching my likes climb and reading my comments didn't compare to Tanner's deep kisses and nights spent cuddling with a giant sleepy bear in front of a crackling fire.

"Get it." He stole a kiss. "I'll give you privacy and get started on lunch." He gave me one last lingering gaze that melted my heart before he walked into the kitchen.

"Hi, Brenda." I tried to sound cheerful.

"Hi, Brenda? Chellie, I've been calling you for days. Your mailbox was full."

"We had a storm. The power was out for three days, and my phone died." This was the truth, but we've had power since yesterday, and I didn't check my messages or return any calls.

"Well, you're going to be glad you picked up. You are back, baby."

"What do you mean?"

"You need to cut your mountain retreat short and come back to the city."

"What? Why?"

"The Kick wants you to endorse their new skincare line."

"What? Like the real Kick."

"Yes, they're willing to move past the New Year's party disaster and work with you again. Everyone loves a comeback story."

"That's crazy."

"No, it's lucrative. So start packing. Also, I managed to book a couple of nightclub appearances. You are not to touch a drop of alcohol," Brenda said. I rolled my eyes.

"But I still have another week here." I glanced at Tanner, standing in front of the stove, holding a spatula. He grinned and winked at me. I returned his smile.

"I'm sorry. Did I slip into a language that you don't understand while I was explaining that you just landed the holy grail of endorsement deals? You can leave the filthy, creature-infested woods and return to civilization."

"I just...I just...I really wanted to stay for the full month." It was all I could think to say. What was I going to tell my manager?

I can't come home yet because I fell in love with a man who is a supernatural creature who can transform into a bear, and I'm his soul mate.

"Chellie. I obviously can't force you to come back, but I would beg you to remember why you went to the woods in the first place. You did it to rehab your image and get your career back on track. You did it. So come back. You can't let these offers sit around. They'll go to someone else. Bank all the money you can while you're still relevant. Call me to let me know you're on your way to the city. Talk later." She hung up.

"Hey, babe. Everything okay?" Tanner said when I slid into one of the kitchen chairs. I nodded and tried to paste on a smile. "I don't believe you."

"Can we talk about it after lunch? I'm hungry."

"You're the boss." He leaned over and kissed me on the head before setting a large bowl in front of me.

"What's this?" I furrowed my brow at him while grinning.

"I know you like salads, so I made a salad for lunch." He grinned proudly. Tanner had lined a bowl with mixed greens, but he topped it with grilled steak, bacon, three types of cheddar cheese, croutons, and ranch dressing. My mother would have cried actual tears if she saw me eating this.

"This looks amazing. Thank you." I grabbed a fork and dug in. It was so good, and I couldn't believe I was giving this up. And for what? The Kick?

"What's going on, mate?" Tanner smiled at me.

"You need to think of a cuter nickname for me." It was a joke, of course. I love the idea of being Tanner's mate, and these last two weeks have been like a dream. Tanner wasn't kidding when he said his job was to take care of me. He spent the previous two weeks doting on me. He cooked for us and ran my baths.

What's more, he valued me as a person. My job wasn't frivolous or silly to him. He took me seriously, and once, after a particularly long day, he told me he was proud of me. I gave him the best night of not having sex after he said that.

I was actually contemplating leaving all that behind. I decided that it would be temporary. I would go for a week, then come back. But come back for how long? What was my long-term solution?

"Chellie?" Tanner squeezed my hand, and I realized that I zoned out.

"Tanner." I decided to rip the Band-Aid off. "My manager called me."

"Brenda?" he asked. He remembered my manager's name. I was leaving a man that actually paid attention when I talked. Memories of Mike's eyes glazing over when I spoke about work flashed in my mind. I pushed them away.

"Yeah. She set up some meetings and appearances for me in the city, and I need to go home." I referred to the city as home, and it felt strange.

Tanner tried to look stoic, but he deflated, and the glitter in his eyes dulled. A tiny crack formed in my heart, and I squeezed his hand.

"I'm leaving for a week, but I'll come right back."

"Will you?" He sounded like he didn't believe me.

"Of course. You're my mate. We're supposed to be together, right?"

"Chellie, have you decided whether or not you want a life with me...here?" He indicated the cabin.

"Yes, and no," I whispered. "I don't know. I think I need more time." I thought I was sure before I spoke to Brenda, offering me opportunities that I'd worked so hard for.

"When are you leaving?"

"I should leave tonight, but I can leave in the morning if you want."

"What do you want?"

"I want to spend as much time with you as I can." I pushed myself away from the table and climbed into his lap.

Tanner stood with me wrapped around his torso and carried me into his bedroom.

9

WHO'S THE BEEF STEW HOTTIE?

"Hey, girl. How are you holding up?" Dawn asked from my armchair.

"I'm fine. I guess I'm just tired."

I'd been back in the city for three days. The meeting with The Kick was great. We all laughed about the party, and I had a cardboard box full of skincare products sitting in the corner of my bedroom and a big fat check sitting in Brenda's office.

"Sure," Dawn said. She didn't believe me, but I was tired. I was tired of being away from Tanner. I'd been calling him and texting him, but all of my efforts to contact him had gone unanswered. I wasn't upset. I called him to let him know I got back to the city safely, and he told me that he'd be away for a few days where I wouldn't be able to reach him, but I tried anyway.

"Well, I finished the website for the lodges. There's also the mockups for the postcards and the brochures. I was hoping you had time to talk about a social media strategy. Are you gonna hire a social media manager? Chellie?"

"What? Um, yeah. I'm gonna help him get set up, but I guess I'll have to hire someone."

"You're in love, aren't you?"

"What?" I looked at Dawn, and she raised her eyebrows. "No," I admitted. "It's worse. It's so much worse."

"What do you mean?"

"This is going to sound crazy because I've only known him for three weeks, but he's my soul mate. I don't think I can live without him."

"And you didn't sleep with him?" She smirked at me.

"No." I laughed and threw a pillow at her.

"So, what's the problem?"

"Can I trust you?"

Dawn dropped her head to the side and glared at me.

"Okay, I'm about to tell you something crazy, but I promise you it's all true. And you can't tell a soul."

"Okay, I'm ready."

I told Dawn everything, and I mean everything. I know I shouldn't have been surprised, but she knew a lot about shifters. Most of this knowledge came from romance novels, but a lot of it was spot on. She whipped out her phone and pulled up a lot of indigenous lore about shapeshifters and skinwalkers to show me. Tears began to roll down my cheeks.

"What?"

I didn't mean to start crying, but something about Dawn's immediate acceptance of my story was something I wasn't prepared for.

"Oh my God, Chellie. You are so soft." She chuckled, but her eyes were welling with tears too. "You know I love you. So what are you going to do about Tanner?"

"I don't know. My work is here, but he'd never survive the city. I don't know how I could make it work and still have my job.

"I think you should talk to your grandmother."

"Nana?"

"She's the one that first told you about shifters. Maybe she knows something that might help you. Maybe don't lead off with the fact that your boyfriend is a bear, but..." She shrugged.

"How are you so okay with this?"

"I don't know. I'm usually pretty open to new concepts. There's so much out there that we don't know. How can we evolve if we're not willing to learn?" She shrugged again. "Also, once you said it, it made perfect sense. All the clues were there."

"What clues?"

"Really? All the bear shit, the way he was hovering and inspecting everything. Typical bear behavior. Not allowing hunters in a resort full of cabins in the mountains. My mind didn't immediately jump to *I bet this dude transforms into a bear at night*, but it fits."

"Thank you, Dawn." I wiped away a tear. She grinned at me. "I'm gonna call my nana, but first, let's look at the stuff you designed. You just gave me an idea for our marketing strategy."

———— •••• ————

"CELESTINE, darling. How long has it been?" My grandmother stood, and her face spread into a brilliant grin, making her look girlish despite her seventy years. Her long glossy silver locks were pulled back in a low chignon.

"Too long, Nana." I wrapped my arms around her shoulders and gently squeezed.

"So, my beautiful girl, what brings you all the way out to Connecticut? I hope my daughter isn't driving you too crazy." She laughed, and I loved that we were on the same page about Mother. It seems so strange to think that the funny, intelligent, strong, and easygoing woman who sat across from me in her parlor raised a woman like her.

"Yes, she is. But that's not why I'm here."

"What is it, darling?"

"Do you remember those bedtime stories you told me when I was little?"

"I believe I told you a lot of stories. You'll need to be more specific."

"The ones about shifters."

Her face perked up, and her eyes darted to my shoulder, where my bite prickled, or maybe I'd imagined it.

"I think we should go for a walk." She rose to her feet. "Stephanie," she called to her house manager, "Celestine and I will have lunch on the veranda."

"Nana, are you sure? It's cold out."

"We'll manage." She grinned at me.

Stephanie nodded and left the room before Nana and I stepped into the chilly air.

"So, what's their name?" She smiled slyly.

"Who?" I asked. Nana turned to face me and tugged at the collar of my sweater, exposing my bite and running her fingertips over the mark. "How did you know?"

She used her index finger to tug at the collar of her turtleneck blouse to expose her own bite. My breath left my body momentarily. Her smile widened.

"Wolf," she said before raising her eyebrows at me in question.

"Bear," I replied. She nodded and hooked her arm in mine and began to stroll past the evergreen trees that lined her sprawling back garden.

"Was grandfather a wolf?" I asked.

"No, your grandfather was a very good man, but he was a man."

"So, who marked you?"

"My soul mate. We met when I was younger than you are now. We fell in love very quickly. He asked me to marry him, but I turned him down."

"If he was your soul mate, why?"

"We were too different. That's what I told myself at the time. Henry was next in line to be the alpha of his pack. Do you remember what an alpha is, dear?"

"Yes," I remembered from Nana's stories. "He's the leader and protector."

"Yes, and if I married him, I would've become the alpha female of the pack. Henry was so sure I could do it. He believed in me, but I didn't believe in myself. I still remember how other members of the pack viewed me. There was even talk of other wolves challenging him for alpha if he married me. I didn't care about myself as much as I cared about how my being in his life hurt him." She sighed, and I could hear the profound sadness in her words.

"My family never liked Henry. He wasn't wealthy, but that didn't matter to me. The only thing that mattered to me was how he made me feel when we were alone, but that's not how a marriage works. At least that's what I thought. So, I left him a note in the middle of the night because I couldn't bear to say goodbye. My parents sent me to Europe to study abroad. I met your grandfather, married him, and you know the rest."

I had no idea my grandmother was so unhappy. My heart ached thinking about how painful it must have been for her. I also ached for my grandfather, who fell in love with a woman who could never love him in return.

"Did you love Grandfather?" I thought about my asking Tanner what would happen if I were married when we met. I wondered if it was possible to love someone who wasn't your soul mate.

"I couldn't." She patted my arm as we strolled. "But I was very fond of Peter. He was a good husband, provider, and father. Unfortunately, my heart belonged to someone else, and it always would."

"What happened to him? Henry?"

"I know he came to my parents and begged them for my whereabouts. I know he tried to find me for a long time. I know he eventually married someone else. I assume she was another wolf shifter." She shrugged, and her voice got smaller as she talked.

"Do you know where he is?"

She shook her head.

"But I know he's still alive."

"How?" I asked.

She touched her bite mark.

"I can still feel him." She got quiet for a long time, and we continued to walk around the yard.

"Nana," I said, and she looked at me. "Do you regret leaving him?"

She patted my hand.

"I don't regret you. I don't regret your mother—she tries her best, you know." She patted my hand. I wondered if some of my mother's insecurities stemmed from her parents' loveless marriage. "Or the wonderful life I had with your grandfather, but if I had it to do all over again, I would have never left that bed. There isn't a day that goes by that I don't miss him. Every morning I wake up and reach for him. So, I guess the answer to your question is yes. I do have regrets."

"Nana." My eyes welled with tears. "It's not too late. Maybe you can find him."

"No, dear," she sighed. "I made my choices. I made the wrong choices for the right reasons, and I have to live with them."

I wrapped her in my arms and squeezed her. We walked to the veranda where lunch waited for us. Stephanie set up portable heaters, and it was surprisingly toasty.

"So, enough about my tragic tale of love and loss. Tell me about your bear. I hope you have photos, but I'm sure you have plenty." She chuckled.

I showed Nana the video of Tanner and me making stew. Then I told her all about our time together on the mountain. The mountain lion attack and my learning how to chop wood.

"I'm happy for you, dear. So, what will you decide?"

There was no decision to make after I heard my grandmother's story. How could I do anything else but find Tanner, wrap myself around him, and never come up for air?

I smiled and kissed her cheek.

"Nana, I have to go. Thank you. I love you."

"Love you too. Good luck!" She winked at me.

I left her on her veranda, sipping tea and absent-mindedly rubbing her shoulder through her sweater.

———— • • • • ————

I CALLED Brenda on my way back to the city.

"Hey, Chellie. What's up?"

"I'm quitting."

"What?"

"I'm quitting."

"Quitting to do what?"

"I took a job as marketing manager for a resort in the Catskills."

"This isn't funny. Did you hit your head?"

"No. I'll honor the rest of my endorsement deals, but once they run out, I'm done. And cancel all of my appearances."

"Chellie, does this have anything to do with the beef stew hottie?"

"Who's the beef stew hottie?"

"Wow. You really haven't been checking your social media. The post with you and the sexy lumberjack making beef stew has gone viral. It's all over Twitter, Facebook, and Snapchat."

I put Brenda on speaker and checked my Instagram. The video of Tanner and me had over forty-two million views after it automatically posted two days ago. I couldn't believe I'd forgotten about it. Of course, people would be going crazy over the sight of me with a new sexy bearded man so soon after my breakup with Mike. For the first time in a long time, the opinions of all those people didn't matter to me. Only one person's opinion mattered.

"Actually, it has everything to do with the beef stew hottie."

"Chellie, please think about this."

"I don't have to think about it. I'm going to make an announcement, but I wanted to give you a heads-up."

"You can't—"

"I'm hanging up, Brenda."

I ended the call. One minute later, my mother called. I let it go to voicemail. Then I turned my phone off and closed my eyes reveling in the peace and quiet.

———— •••• ————

WHEN I GOT BACK to my apartment, I was intent on packing as much stuff as I could get into two suitcases and hauling ass upstate when I was met at the door by Dawn.

"What's up?"

"There's someone here to see you."

"Shit. Is it my mother?"

"No," she said deadpan. "It's a giant bearded man."

I deflated. Mike was the second to last person I wanted to see.

"It's not Mike," she said, correctly reading my expression. My heart thudded and stopped.

"What?"

She grinned, and I took off, running towards my bedroom. Tanner was sitting in my armchair when I opened the door. My heart leaped in my chest, and my face spread into a wide grin. He jumped to his feet when he saw me and I ran into his arms.

"What are you doing here?"

"I thought that would be obvious." His beard and mustache twitched.

"How? I thought you have to shift every night. Are you leaving tonight?"

"Well, I took a few days as a bear, hoping it would mean that I could stay here with you for a couple of days."

My eyes welled with tears. That was why he didn't answer my calls and texts.

"You did that for me?"

"I would do anything for you." He leaned down and kissed me. "So, can I crash here for a few days?" He grinned at me.

"No," I said and grinned right back at him.

"No?" He furrowed his brow at me.

"No, you can't stay here because we're going home right now." I grabbed my suitcase out of the closet and started filling it with clothes.

"Home?"

"Black Bear Mountain Lodges."

10

THOSE BADGERS DESERVE TO SEE ME
AT MY BEST

We made the trip up the New York State Thruway in Tanner's pickup truck, and I wished we'd hired a driver because it meant waiting another four hours before I could jump him. That didn't stop Tanner's hand from traveling up my thigh and using his thick fingers to caress my sex through my jeans. We made out at every stoplight. By the time we got to the cabin, I was hot enough to start a fire without a match.

"Fuck, I missed you, mate," Tanner growled into my neck as he scooped me into his arms and ran towards the cabin. He put me down so he could take off his coat and lock the door. When he turned around, I was completely naked.

"Shit." His eyes raked over my body, taking in every fold and curve. "Do you want to go to the bedroom?" he whispered, not meeting my eye. I shook my head and crooked my finger at him. He stalked towards me, snatching the giant quilt off the couch and laying it out on the floor before the fireplace.

"Come here, mate," I whispered with my arms outstretched. "Claim me."

His eyes flashed, and he closed the distance between us in two long strides. Tanner's strong arms wrapped around my waist, and he covered my mouth with his in a hungry kiss. I was home, not just on this mountain and in Tanner's cabin. My home was in his arms.

I broke away from him and started tugging at his clothes. He tore off his shirts, and I dropped to my knees and clawed at his belt buckle. His jeans and boxers dropped to his ankles, and before he could step out of them, I gripped and stroked his shaft, planting gentle kisses on the thick crown.

"Jesus Christ, that feels so good." He moaned as I brought my fists apart and together, massaging his length using my saliva as lubricant.

"I had a good teacher." I smiled up at him. I was, of course, using Tanner's wood-chopping technique to stroke him before I closed my lips over the thick head of his cock and began to suck. Tanner let out a guttural growl, and his fingers flew to my hair, pushing himself deeper into me until I was nearly swallowing him. I wrapped my arms around his waist, dug my fingers into the rigid flesh of his ass, pulling us closer together until I was gagging. My eyes began to sting with tears, and I felt his pubic hair tickling my nose and lips.

"Oh, fuck, Chellie. Fuck, I love you," Tanner gritted as I bobbed back and forth on his cock. I used one hand to caress his balls, and they tightened in my hands before Tanner's body tensed, his grip tightened on my hair, and he shot two ropes of hot thick cum down my throat. I sat back on my heels, still swallowing. Tanner collapsed on the quilt next to me, drew me into his arms and wiped away the tears mixed with mascara on my cheeks. His chest rose and fell in deep breaths.

"Tanner, you just told me you loved me," I whispered, my face inches from his.

"I did," he said with a small nod.

"Did you say it because I had your dick in my mouth or—"

Tanner interrupted me with a huge bark of laughter and rolled me on top of him.

"I said it because I love you." He kissed me. "I love you when you have my dick in your mouth." He kissed me again. "I love you when I have my face between your legs." He nipped me on the neck. "I love you when you're arguing with me. I love you when you're spending forty-five minutes putting on makeup for a hike through the woods."

"Hey, those badgers deserve to see me at my best." I giggled and planted a kiss on one of his pecs. A deep chuckle rumbled in his chest against my cheek.

"I love you when you're making me laugh."

"I love you when you're telling me how much you love me."

"Then, you're going to love me a lot." He rolled on top of me, and I wrapped my legs around his waist. Tanner's rigid shaft glided between the slick lips of my center, and I ached for him to enter me.

"Tanner, please."

"Chellie, condoms..." Tanner started to pull away, and I tightened my legs around his waist.

"When's the last time you've been tested?" I asked.

"I haven't been with anyone in over a year, and I've been tested twice since then. I'm negative for everything, well, everything a shifter can get," Tanner responded. Wow, he hasn't had sex in a year. He might actually kill me tonight, and I couldn't wait.

"I haven't had sex in four months, and my last appointment was two months ago. I'm negative too."

"Chellie, we should think about birth control."

"Tanner, I love you, and I'm never leaving you again. I want a life with you and a family in this cabin. I want these woods. Maybe not the mountain lions. But most of all, I want this...us." I tangled my fingers in his beard, and he opened his mouth to speak. I pressed the pad of my fingertip over his lips and said, "Yes, I'm sure. I'm still on the pill, but whatever happens, happens. I'm ready."

He lowered his face to mine and devoured me in a hungry kiss.

"God, I fucking love you," he whispered.

"I love you too, Tanner," I whispered back and dug my heels in the firm flesh of his ass. "Now, show me how much you love me."

Tanner reached between our bodies to guide himself into me. He dipped into my wetness, then slid his thick crown over and across my clit before sinking into me again, a little further each time. I felt like I was being teased and tortured until he finally gave me his full length, making me groan in pleasure.

Tanner blanketed me with his massive body, careful not to crush me with his full weight as he rocked his hips back and forth, filling me.

"Oh my God, Tanner. Yes, fuck me. You feel so good." I moaned and whimpered in pleasure as Tanner's warm breath caressed my neck. He dug his fingertips into the flesh of my thighs wrapped around his waist.

"I've been waiting so long for you, mate," he growled in my neck. It showed in Tanner's lovemaking. He was tender and gentle with the fury of pent-up passion bubbling under the surface. I wanted that passion. I wanted everything he had to give me.

"Now you have me, Tanner," I moaned. "So, take me."

His eyes flashed the golden brown I recognized from his bear form, and he stopped, looking down at me.

"I don't want to hurt you, Chellie."

"You won't." I touched his cheek. "I'm tougher than I look, remember." I smiled at him. "Now, fuck me like you really want to."

His eyes flashed and darkened before he leaned down and took my mouth in a bruising kiss. He pulled away with my bottom lip between his teeth.

Tanner's massive thighs spread, opening me further for him. He grabbed one of my knees and pressed it into my chest before lengthening his stroke and quickening his pace. Bear-like grunts erupted from his chest as our hips crashed together over and over. Unintelligible moans and cries escaped my lips as I dug my nails into my mate's shoulder.

"Yes. Yes. Oh, fuck yes, baby. Fuck me just like this."

Tanner answered me with a growl before withdrawing himself and flipping me onto my stomach. I could already tell that I was going to be sore tomorrow, but the exquisite endorphin-filled mix of pleasure and pain was worth it. Plus, I knew my mate would spend the whole day taking care of me.

He pulled me onto my hands and knees before again gliding the head of his cock over my entrance.

"Are you still with me, mate?"

I nodded my head.

"I didn't hear that?" He punctuated his question with a loud slap that stung my ass cheek and sent a streak of lightning between my legs, causing all of the muscles there to clench and relax.

"Fuck, yes. Always. Please, hurry." I tried to wiggle and back my hips into him, but he held me steady, carefully guiding himself into me until our hips connected. He began to rock back and forth, slowly at first, then gradually picking up speed.

"Dammit, Chellie. You feel so fucking good. So fucking good." He gripped my shoulder with one large hand and gripped my waist with the other as he drove himself into me. I could feel the sweat pouring off of my body, and my elbows started to tremble. "Fuck. It's too good. I can't..."

He reached around my waist and cupped one of my breasts as he pulled my back into his chest, pumping his hips upwards as he continued to fuck me until I was boneless. The thick fingers of the hand that wasn't pinching my nipple reached between my legs and began to strum my clit, throwing me into a frenzy.

He let out a final growl before thrusting into me and once again digging his teeth into my shoulder, retracing his mark from a different angle. Tanner's hands and teeth drove me to an earth-shattering climax as I felt the muscles of his body clench and relax. His hot, thick release leaked from where our bodies connected, coating our thighs as I came down from my orgasm. My chest heaved as I sucked in lungfuls of oxygen.

Tanner still held me against him, slowly rocking himself in and out of my body while soothing his bite mark with his tongue and gentle kisses.

"I love you, Chellie. I love you so much. You're mine. You'll always be mine."

"Good," I sighed as he lifted me off of him and lowered me onto the quilt, "because you are never getting rid of me now." I chuckled, and it made my muscles ache. "Ow."

"Are you okay, babe?" he asked, lazily dragging his fingertips over my sweat-drenched body.

"No," I laughed, "and I never want to be again."

———— · · · · ————

TANNER MADE US DINNER, and afterward, he ran us a bath in his giant tub where we soaked, and he massaged my sore muscles. I could really get used to this.

"Hey, baby," I asked as he dragged a giant soapy sponge over my back. "Did I tell you that I think I figured out what you should do with the resort?"

"No." He kissed my shoulder. "But, I get the feeling you're about to."

I chuckled and splashed him.

"Well, you and Dawn actually inspired my idea."

"Oh yeah?"

"When you told me how hard it was for you and your parents as a kid. But you had this place and people who understood what you needed. Then Dawn told me everything she knew about shifters, and I thought, *how many others are out there?* How many people are there like you? They should have a place to go and *be themselves* for a little while, right?"

He let go of the sponge and wrapped his arms around my waist pulling me into him. He was hard again and pressing into my lower back.

"You're amazing. I don't know what I did to deserve you."

I spun in his arms to face him.

"Fate." I wrapped my arms around his neck and kissed him.

"I want you again." He reached between us and brushed a fingertip over my clit make me shiver.

"I think the front entrance is out of commission for the night, but the back door..." I waggled my eyebrows and moved his hand to cup my backside.

"Fuck, Chellie..." He groaned and kissed me again.

I grinned at him and tucked my bottom lip between my teeth.

"Yes, please."

THE END

11

SHIFT YOUR PERSPECTIVE
EPILOGUE

This epilogue takes place after the paperback exclusive bonus epilogue: Grin & Bear It.*

*

———————— • • • • ————————

"Good morning, mama bear. How are you feeling?" I reached around and palmed my mate's round belly and planted a kiss on her lips.

"Huge. Horny. Hungry." She pouted at me. I chuckled and kissed her again.

"I can help with two of those things." I raised my eyebrows at her. "But you, my love, are beautiful. What do you want for breakfast?"

"Sex first." She grabbed the collar of my t-shirt and pulled me in for a kiss. I sunk my teeth into her bottom lip just hard enough to leave an imprint but not break the skin and soothed the marks with my tongue. I kissed and nibbled my way across her throat. My fist opened and closed as I pulled her nightgown over her hips. Her familiar and enticing scent invaded my nostrils, spreading warmth in my chest and sending blood further south.

"You didn't wear panties to bed again," I whispered in her ear, sliding a finger between her slick folds.

"Yes, I did," she moaned with a little chuckle. "You took them off, remember?"

"Oh, yeah. I did, didn't I?" I grinned at her before making my way down her body, planting more kisses. I pressed my lips to her belly before tickling the soft skin of her inner thighs with my beard.

"Oooh, Tanner," she pleaded. "Don't tease me."

I pressed my nose into the downy tuft of hair between her legs and inhaled. My mate smelled delicious, but she tasted even better when I dragged my tongue through her opening. She moaned loudly and rocked her hips to meet my lips.

"Are you sure this is okay, so close to your due date?" I angled my head to peer at her around her belly.

"Yes, stop asking me that. Anna says it's fine, and she's the shifter pregnancy expert, not you. Now, get back down there."

I listened to the boss. Her skin trembled under the caress of my palms as I kissed every inch of her delicate flesh until I reached her center. I once again inhaled the sweet musky scent of her arousal before pressing my tongue into her core and devouring every drop of her delicious nectar while she moaned in ecstasy.

She came on my tongue. Then about fifteen minutes later, she came in my arms while riding my dick, and a few minutes after that, I came in her mouth.

We collapsed onto the bed. I pulled my mate into my arms and stroked her hair. She smelled like shampoo, sex and me. I loved covering her in my scent, a reminder that I was hers and always would be.

"Breakfast?"

"I would kill for some salmon sushi."

I laughed.

"You know you can't have that. How about pancakes, eggs, and bacon."

"I've been craving raw fish for months."

"This time next month, you can eat all the sushi you want."

"Your mom said that after the baby comes, I won't want it anymore." She frowned at me. "She also said the rapid healing thing will stop too." Chellie cut herself shaving her legs a few months ago. When it healed in twenty minutes, we called my mother, who referred us to the shifter midwife, Anna, who delivered me. That's how we found out that we were expecting a cub.

My mom and Chellie have gotten close over the last year, and I'm glad because she barely speaks to her own mother. Once she found out we were having a baby, she really leaned on Mom for support and advice. Of course, my mother was thrilled to have a grandchild, though she wished Chellie and I would get married. We'll get around to it, but we're not in a rush.

Between me, my family, her grandmother, and Dawn, my mate has plenty of love and support, but I know she wished things were better with her own mother.

"I guess I can settle for pancakes." She kissed me. "Lots of honey?"

"Whatever my mate wants."

———— •••• ————

"BLACK BEAR MOUNTAIN LODGES. Shift your perspective and have a transformative experience. How can I help you?" Chellie winked at me while holding the phone receiver to her ear.

"No. We don't allow hunting... Nope. No exceptions. Thanks for calling." She hung up and rolled her eyes at me. "Kiss me, handsome."

I leaned forward and kissed her over the reception desk.

"Why are you answering phones?"

"Lindsay needed a break." The phone chirped. "Hold on, sexy... Black Bear Mountain Lodges. Shift your perspective and have a transformative experience. How can I help you?" She paused for a long time nodding. "Of course. I think little Bradley would love it here. Lots of space and privacy... Mmm-hmm..." She held the mouthpiece away from her and whispered to me. "Human mom. Wolf cub."

She returned her attention to her call. "I understand. I'm expecting a little bear cub any day now." She laughed and winked at me. Lindsay walked in. "Okay, I'm gonna hand you off to our reservations specialist, Lindsay... Great! You too... Oh, thank you. We're excited. Okay, Meghan, here's Lindsay." She passed the phone off and waddled around the counter to wrap her arms around me and pressed her cheek to my chest.

"Did my nana get here yet?"

"That's why I came to get you." I scooped her into my arms and carried her to the truck. "Her driver called. They're about a half hour away." Chellie's grandmother is coming to stay with us until the baby is born and a couple of weeks after.

We pulled up to the cabin five minutes later, and I pulled her into my arms and walked in the living room, carefully setting her on the couch and covering her with the quilt.

"Are you going to stop carrying me everywhere once the baby comes?" She grinned at me as I made my way to the kitchen.

"Probably not." I grinned at her as I turned on the stove.

I returned with a mug of tea. Chellie sighed as she snuggled beside me when I joined her on the couch.

"Did you put—"

"Extra honey?" I kissed her. "Yes, but you're switching to water after this one. Anna says you should watch your sugar intake."

"Boo." She sipped her tea. "Mmmm. Perfect."

I reached out and covered her belly with my hand. Our cub responded with a thump on my palm. A year ago, I wouldn't believe I'd be sitting here. After thirty years—the last five spent living alone on this mountain—I'd given up on finding the mate my grandfather promised me, then one day she showed up. Celestine Woods wasn't what I thought I wanted, but she turned out to be everything I needed.

"Whoa." I looked at the woman who'd become my entire world. She was gazing at me with tears in her eyes.

"What's wrong, babe?"

"Nothing. Absolutely nothing. Everything is perfect." A tear spilled from her eye, and I brushed it away with the pad of my thumb. "I wish I had a picture of this."

"Where's your phone?"

A slow grin spread over my mate's face, which gave way to belly laughs.

"You know what?" she asked when her laughter subsided. "I have no idea."

GRIN & BEAR IT: I
BONUS EPILOGUE: CHELLIE

This paperback exclusive epilogue takes place before the epilogue: Shift Your Perspective.*

*

"ARE YOU SURE ABOUT THIS, BABY?" I teetered on a stepstool in my stilettos as I reached out to straighten Tanner's bowtie. "I can make up an excuse if you don't feel comfortable. Nana will understand."

"Yes. I'm sure, beautiful." He leaned forward to kiss me, testing the durability of my no-smudge lipstick. "Your Nana is important to you, and you're important to me. So, your Nana is also important to me."

He winked at me. My face split into an involuntary grin, and Tanner's words elicited a warm tingling feeling in my chest. God, I loved this man so much.

"You know my mother is going to be there," I said in a groan. I hoped to keep Tanner away from Evelyn Woods Bennett Sumner Tobin Walker as long as humanly possible. He was something good and pure in my life. I've never been happier than I have in these last few months with him living in semi-seclusion, a far cry from my life in Manhattan. Unfortunately, happiness wasn't an emotion my mother had any use for.

She had also never gotten over my decision to quit modeling and shut down wealthy marriage prospects to move into the woods with whom she calls a "mountain man." It's not exactly an insult, but coming from my mother, most things are.

We put the finishing touches on our wardrobes in preparation for our long drive to Connecticut for my grandmother's annual birthday gala.

Nana started throwing herself birthday parties the year after my grandfather died. I just assumed that she did it out of loneliness because she never seemed to enjoy them. Now, I knew that my grandmother loved someone else and married my grand-father as a rebound. When I think back on the parties, they seemed almost Gatsby-ish, like she was waiting for some mystery guest to show up. Maybe that was true.

"Yes, mate, I know your mother will be there." Tanner leaned down and kissed me again. "You warned me." He gave me a smile and let out a soft chuckle. "Did you forget that I fought a mountain lion? Your mother can't be worse than that."

I wasn't so sure about that.

"Okay. All done, handsome." I patted the knotted strip of black fabric at his throat. He hit me with a gorgeous grin that showcased the tiny gap in his two front teeth before he helped me climb down from the stepstool. I'd never seen Tanner in a suit before. We had to find a tailor in a town forty-five minutes away who could make a tuxedo in his size. It fit him perfectly. My giant James Bond was as sexy as ever, but I still preferred him in denim and flannel.

Who was I kidding?

I would take my mountain man any way I could get him.

"How do you feel?" I asked as I smoothed my palms over the lapels of his jacket.

"It's not the most comfortable thing I've ever worn, but for you—" he kissed my forehead, "I'll deal with it...for how long?" He raised a questioning eyebrow at me and tugged on the sleeves of his dress shirt.

"Just a few hours, I promise. Plus, Dawn and her family will be there. So, it won't be like I'm the only person you know." Dawn was one of my three favorite people in the world.

"Yeah. I like Dawn." He brushed a stray lock of hair from my forehead.

"She likes you too." I gave him a wink and pulled him down for another kiss. "And if you think you're uncomfortable, I'm the one wearing this tight ass dress and four-inch heels."

"You look delicious, baby." He shot me a devilish grin and reached out to touch my cheek, dragging the pad of his finger across my chin, down my throat, over the golden-brown bite mark he gave me on my shoulder and along the globes of my breasts that were pushed up by the bodice of the dress.

"Tanner?" I said in a small whisper. His touch blazed a trail of heat across my skin that quickly spread to other parts of my body. "What are you doing?"

"My favorite thing." He slowly lowered himself to his knees and ran his giant calloused palms up my shins and my thighs underneath the skirt of my dress.

"Do you mean the thing you did when we woke up, twice after lunch, and another time in the shower while we were getting ready?" I asked with a mischievous grin.

"Yes. That thing." He scooped me under the thighs, wrapped my legs around his waist, and tossed me on our bed.

"Tanner," I said with a scream and a giggle as I bounced on the mattress. "You are going to wrinkle my dress and ruin my makeup."

"So, does that mean I should stop?" he asked with a raised eyebrow as his palm slid up my thigh, and he brushed a thumb over my clit through my panties. He had no intention of stopping, and I had no intention of letting him.

"I'd be very pissed if you did."

"That's what I thought." He hooked his index fingers into the elastic waistband of my thong and slid it down my legs, then he opened my sex and planted the gentlest kiss on my clit before sucking it between his lips.

"God, I fucking love you," I moaned as I reached between my legs and pulled the thin black elastic out of Tanner's hair, releasing his bun so I could tangle my fingers in his wavy locks as he tasted and teased me to another earth-shattering orgasm. "Fuck me, baby. Please. I need you."

He picked his head up, his mustache and beard glistening with the evidence of my ever-present need for him, his face serious. "Do we have time for that?"

"I. Don't. Give a fuck." I shifted my weight onto my elbows so I could almost sit up to look at him, still kneeling between my legs. "I need you. Now. Right now."

Tanner didn't have to be told twice. He unbuttoned his tuxedo pants, and they slid down his legs with his boxer briefs. His long thick cock sprung free, erect and bobbing with a glistening bead of pre-cum. I reached out, wrapped my palm around his shaft, and smoothed the tip of my thumb across the tip, swiping the sticky bead before tucking my thumb in my mouth and sucking.

"So fucking good," Tanner whispered as he crawled between my legs and sheathed himself in one torturously slow stroke. "You feel so fucking good." He withdrew his hips before sliding into me again and again, slowly at first, then picking up speed. My moans increased as Tanner worked himself into a frenzy between my legs. He pressed his face into my hair, and I could feel his hot breath caressing my scalp as he grunted his way to his own release. I wrapped my legs around his waist, digging the heel of my stiletto into the firm muscles of his ass, urging him deeper and deeper with every thrust. I angled my hips up to meet his with every stroke, and I came again, screaming his name and telling him how much I loved him and how much I needed him.

"Fuck, Chellie. Fuck." Tanner rammed his hips into mine with one final bruising thrust. His body tensed and relaxed, then tensed and relaxed again, before he collapsed on top of me, planting delicate kisses on my neck and my chin. He sucked my ear lobe into his mouth, gently dragging his teeth across it. "I love you so much. I love you so much, precious. You're mine. I love you," he murmured softly as he held me against him while we recovered from our orgasms.

"I love you too, baby." I reached over and tangled my fingertips in his beard and gently scratched while I gazed into his deep brown eyes. "We better get up soon. I have to put myself back together, and we have a long drive since someone insisted on not hiring a car." I narrowed my eyes at him with a smirk.

"You're *my* mate," Tanner said and gave me a gentle kiss. "That means I take care of you. If we're going somewhere, I take you."

"Okay, He-Man," I mocked him in a deep goofy voice. "Let's get up and get out of here before we're not able to get out of this bed."

"I wouldn't mind that." He sat up, left the bed, and returned with a damp cloth.

"Me, neither," I chuckled as he began to wipe between my legs. "But I don't want to disappoint my grandmother, and in a few hours, we'll be right back here."

"I like the sound of that." Tanner leaned down and kissed me. His breath was heavy with my scent.

"Babe, I'm not complaining," I shot him a grin, "but you might want to brush your teeth before I introduce you to my grandmother."

Tanner chuckled and shook his head before hoisting me over his shoulder and carrying me to the bathroom.

GRIN & BEAR IT: II
BONUS EPILOGUE: CHELLIE

"Celestine, darling." My grandmother rushed towards me and wrapped her arms around my shoulders. She wore a long-sleeved floor-length silver gown. She had her equally silver hair pulled up into an elegant chignon held in place with a diamond-encrusted barrette. She looked luminous and much younger than her seventy-one years.

"I am so happy to see you, and I'm so glad you could make it." Her eyes roved over to Tanner, who, despite being dressed in the uniform of the uptight Connecticut elite, looked extremely out of place. It made my heart flutter, and I squeezed his hand. "And I'm very happy to see you." She gave my mate a radiant smile and extended her hand. Tanner released my hand to grab my Nana's and leaned down to kiss it.

"Happy Birthday, Mrs. Woods." Tanner smiled nervously at Nana. "You have a lovely home; thank you for having us."

Nana shot me a look and smiled before turning her gaze back to Tanner. "Please, call me Patricia or Nana. Mrs. Woods makes me sound like a stuffy old matron." She chuckled genially. "I'm so glad that you were able to make it. And thank you for making my granddaughter so happy." She winked at me, and Tanner slid his palm around my waist and squeezed.

"Nana, has Mother arrived?" I decided to rip off the bandage as quickly as possible. The sooner Tanner met my mother and got it out of the way, the sooner we could enjoy the rest of the party. I planned on spending the rest of the night in Tanner's arms or chatting with my best friend, who had sent a text that she was five minutes away.

"Why, yes, she is," Nana said. "She and Richard arrived about a half-hour before you did." Richard Walker was my mother's fourth husband. He seemed like a perfectly nice guy, but I didn't know him very well, and I suspected that my mother didn't either.

"Well, I should go find her and say hello." I pasted on a fake smile that my grandmother could see right through. She signaled a passing server and grabbed a glass of champagne from their tray. She handed it to me with a wink.

"Good luck, dear," she said before craning her neck up to look at Tanner. "It was so lovely to meet you, and I hope we get a chance to chat before the night is over."

"Yes, ma'am."

———— • • • • ————

I GRIPPED Tanner's hand like it was my lifeline, because it was, as I gently led him through the crowd while scanning the room for my mother. I found her with her palm pressed over her chest in the middle of her patented fake laugh while chatting with the woman I knew was the wife of a local senator. Richard stood beside her, chatting with the woman's husband.

I knew the exact moment when she spotted me. Her

expression faltered slightly when her eyes landed on Tanner, a very tall, broad, muscular man in a tuxedo with his long hair pulled into a bun and a long but neatly groomed beard. She continued her conversation with the senator's wife, and I knew that she silently hoped that Tanner and I wouldn't interrupt her because then, she'd have to introduce us. After a deep, cleansing breath and a gulp of my champagne, I walked up to her and rubbed my palm over her bare shoulder.

"Mother!" I exclaimed. I had many motives for greeting her this way. One: I hoped she could keep her insults and barbs to a minimum if she had an audience; two: she didn't relish the thought of people knowing that she had a twenty-eight-year-old daughter; and three: the opportunity to embarrass my mother and poke a hole in her nauseating façade of perfection never ceased to give me a small thrill.

"Celestine," my mother replied, pasting on a smile that showed way too many teeth. "How lovely of you to finally make it." She flicked an almost imperceptible glance at her watch.

Welp! That was insult number one out of the way. That wasn't so bad. I took another sip of my champagne.

"I hope that's your first glass of champagne." And there was number two. My mother never let me forget the mortifying way I'd rung in the new year. I couldn't regret it because if it hadn't happened, I would have never met Tanner. "And who is your...friend?"

Lucky number three. She knew that I'd been living with Tanner in the Catskill Mountains for the last few months. She also knew that he was more than a friend, way more.

"Mother." I gripped Tanner's hand and pulled him forward. "This is Tanner, my *boyfriend*." I put extra emphasis on the word 'boyfriend,' and my mother's small scowl let me know that it had the intended effect. It felt strange calling Tanner my boyfriend because he felt like so much more, but we weren't married, we weren't engaged, and calling him my fated mate would've led to more questions. I glanced up at Tanner, and he smiled.

"Well," my mother bristled. "Tanner, it's a pleasure to finally meet you. Celestine speaks of nothing else," she added sardonically.

"Likewise, ma'am," Tanner said with a small nod and the same sardonic tone that I know my mother picked up on, and I couldn't be more proud.

Her eyes narrowed slightly at Tanner before she turned her attention to the senator and his wife.

"Marissa, John, this is my daughter Celestine and her...boyfriend... Tanner, was it?" She knew it was.

Tanner smiled and extended his hand, gripping the senator's and giving it a firm shake.

"Now, that's one hell of grip, young man." The senator laughed jovially and mimicked a grimace while comically flexing his fingers after Tanner's shake.

"Thank you, sir." Tanner let out a hearty chuckle before he turned his attention to his wife, grabbing her hand and placing a delicate kiss on her knuckle.

"A pleasure meeting you, ma'am." This time he actually sounded like he meant it, not like when he greeted my mother. Marissa giggled in response. An actual giggle. I glanced at my mother, and she definitely noticed.

"So, Tanner." Richard stepped forward and extended his hand. "Glad to finally meet you." He smiled and shook hands with my boyfriend and, upon catching the glare from my mother, quickly dropped Tanner's hand, cleared his throat, and took a step back with a small smile and a curt nod.

"So, what kind of business are you in, Tanner?" the senator asked. My mother grimaced again.

"Well—" Tanner began.

"Tanner is in real estate and hospitality," I chimed in. "He owns an amazing resort in the Catskill Mountains. There's a lot of land and plenty of quaint and cozy cabins. There's even a lake with a waterfall." I squeezed his hand and looked up, and he smiled down at me.

"Sounds beautiful," Marissa mused. "Maybe we should go visit, John. What do you think?"

"That's not a bad idea, Mimi. I haven't been hunting in a while. Sounds like a nice trip."

I felt Tanner's muscles tense, and his hand tightened around my fingers.

"Actually, we don't allow hunters on the land. It's protected property... But no less beautiful," I quickly added and felt the grip on my hand loosen slightly.

"No hunters, eh?" The senator crossed his arms and stroked his chin. "I bet that cuts into a lot of your business."

"Ah, yes," my mother chimed in. She had carefully followed our conversation with the senator and his wife but didn't participate until she found the perfect opportunity to strike. "How *is* business?"

"It's steady," I said, glaring at her. It was a bit of a sore spot with Tanner. He constantly worried about being able to provide for me and any children we might have. I told him that he didn't have to worry, but asking my mate not to worry about me was like asking the sun not to rise. "But we're planning a huge renovation and marketing push, so we expect to be really busy by this time next year," I blurted out in response to my mother's withering gaze. I hadn't actually discussed these plans with Tanner.

"A huge renovation?" My mother asked. "That sounds expensive. How do you plan to fund such an exorbitant endeavor?" She glared at me, and I knew deep down inside that she knew the answer but didn't dare say it in front of the senator and his wife.

"We've managed to secure an investor who is very excited about the project and devoted to the success of the resort." Tanner's hand slackened even more around mine. He and my mother were on the same page. This was something else that I hadn't discussed with him. I'd planned to, but I was looking for the right time. I could feel the side of my face heat up where he must have been staring daggers at me, but I couldn't break eye contact with my mother.

"Well, that sounds just wonderful." Marissa clapped her hands together. She had clearly picked up on the tension between the three of us and was planning an elegant, well-rehearsed escape that only the wives of politicians can master. "John and I would love to attend the grand opening, and if you're looking for any new investors, please reach out to us. We love to help young entrepreneurs." She touched her husband on the shoulder. "Darling, I think I see the Covingtons. We should go say hello." She turned to my mother. "Evelyn, Richard, always a pleasure to see you. Celestine and Tanner, lovely to meet you." She linked her arms with her husband, and they turned and slowly moved away from us, being swallowed by the crowd, and we watched them leave. They were an invisible barrier of civility, and now, they'd disappeared.

"Well, now it makes sense." My mother replaced her cool and calm demeanor with a predatory glare as she glanced between me and Tanner. "*You* will be funding this little enterprise." Her gaze settled on me.

Tanner still hadn't spoken, and I wondered if he was in shock. Our hands were still linked, but he felt miles away.

"It's not a *little* enterprise," I spat out. "It's my future, and it's my money. I *earned* it." I cast a glance at Richard, who was suddenly very interested in his gold cufflinks. My mother narrowed her eyes at the barb.

"You *earned* it by photographing yourself using face cream and eating prawns in Barcelona. And that money won't last forever. Especially if you're frittering it away on frivolous pursuits. Were you planning on draining your trust fund, too?"

"Happiness is not a frivolous pursuit, Mother." I dropped Tanner's hand, and my heart clenched at how very little resistance he gave me because, by this point, he was barely holding it. I pointed a finger at my mother's chest. I ignored her comment about my trust fund. Somehow, it was also my fault that my grandfather left me more money in his will. I shook with rage.

"Happiness is the most frivolous pursuit," my mother retorted. "Your father and I were happy... until we weren't. Then, I was left on my own with a child and no way to support it."

I also ignored the fact that she just called me an *it* and focused on her remarks about her's and my father's doomed relationship, which she only mentioned during arguments.

"Oh, Evie." My grandmother appeared out of nowhere before I could reply, and the tension was so thick, you could cut it with a knife. "Always so dramatic." She rolled her eyes. "It's not as if you and Celestine were living on the streets. I think it's wonderful that my granddaughter has found true love. It's rare. It's precious, and it shouldn't be taken for granted."

She took a glass of champagne from a passing server and took a sip.

"I was very sorry about the end of your relationship with Celestine's father, but you've managed to find love again." She nodded her head towards Richard, and though her remarks didn't carry an ounce of sarcasm, it was an unspoken understanding between the three of us that my mother hadn't married Richard for love, and he didn't seem to mind. "And this is my birthday party, and I will not have you upsetting my guests." She smiled, took another sip of her champagne, and turned to Tanner and me.

"Celestine, why don't you take Tanner for a walk and show him the back garden? There's an especially densely packed tree-lined pass at the far corner of the property. Very secluded. I find it to be incredibly...transformative." She gave her eyebrows a little raise and flicked a glance at Tanner, whose expression was blank, but I felt the anger rolling off of him in waves. It made my stomach sink. I gave my grandmother a grateful smile and nodded my understanding.

I slipped my hand into Tanner's again, and he allowed me to lead him towards the back door of the great room and out of the house.

GRIN & BEAR IT: III
BONUS EPILOGUE: CHELLIE

"**I**'m so sorry," I called to Tanner as I struggled to keep up with him in my heels. Tanner took long, quick strides towards the far corner of the back garden. I kicked off my heels and slipped my wrist through the straps while I hustled to catch up.

When we were far enough away from the house to not be seen, he loosened his tie and tossed it over his shoulder. I picked it up. His jacket came next, followed by his dress shirt, his undershirt, and his pants, and by the time we got deep into the dense thicket of trees towards the edge of grandmother's property, Tanner was only in his boxer briefs.

That would've been hot if he wasn't so furious at me and I wasn't so consumed with guilt. I'd always planned on using my money to renovate Black Bear Mountain Lodges. I had plenty, but I needed time to persuade Tanner to let me. Then, the first time he was introduced to my mother, she immediately accused him of using me for my money, something that couldn't be further from the truth.

When he finally stopped and turned to look at me, his chest was heaving, his face reddened.

"I'm so sorry. Please talk to me," I pleaded.

He sucked in a deep breath, and his lips parted as if he were about to say something. I held my breath. Then, he closed his mouth, and shook his head. He kicked his boxers off and within seconds, his bear took his skin, and he bounded into the night. Tanner left me in the woods alone, barefoot, and holding a pile of giant clothes. I leaned against a nearby tree trunk, sank to the ground, and cried.

"That looked intense." Dawn's voice called to me, and I looked up to find her standing a few feet away with her arms crossed. She wore a strapless yellow jumpsuit that perfectly complemented her dark golden-brown complexion. She'd gotten her hair braided for the summer and pulled them up into a giant bun on the top of her head. Her heels were also doing double duty as bracelets and she was out of breath. "Your grandmother said that you might need me."

"She was right. Did you just get here?" I asked and she nodded. I let out a sigh and looked towards the cluster of trees where Tanner had disappeared. "I really fucked up." I told Dawn about the argument with my mother and how I slipped, telling her that I planned to pay to renovate Tanner's resort without discussing it with him first.

"Well, your first mistake was letting your mom bait you like that." She walked over to the tree and sat next to me. She picked up one of Tanner's giant shoes, turned it from side to side, and eyed me with a mischievous grin. "Damn, girl."

"Shut up," I said, trying to suppress a smile.

"I will not." She elbowed me in the ribs, and I started laughing.

"What am I gonna do, Dawn?" I hugged Tanner's pile of clothes to my chest and inhaled his earthy scent, mixed with the cologne I bought him for his birthday. "I love him so much, and I want to make him happy. I know he wants to make me happy, and he feels like it's his job as my fated mate, but aren't we in this together? Aren't we supposed to make each other happy?"

"So, why didn't you tell him that?" she asked, still holding his shoe, for some reason.

"I planned to. He just gets really defensive whenever I try to do anything for him or us. I never thought I would have someone in my life that loves me so much. This is something that I can do for him and us. I think the only thing he loves more than me is that land, and he's so proud of it. I want it to be the best it can be. What's the point of having all this money if I can't use it to make the man I love happy? I was just trying to find a way get around his stubborn pride and explain it to him in a way he'd understand. Then my mother started talking down to him in front of Richard and the senator and his wife. I had to say something. I had to defend him."

"Were you worried about defending Tanner or defending yourself?" She tilted her head, and her eyebrows were raised when I turned to look at her.

Bingo.

My mother drove me crazy, and I knew that she had her own issues, but for some reason— that over a decade of therapy hadn't uncovered—her opinion was important to me, especially when it came to the most important person in my life, Tanner. I don't know why, but for once, I wanted her approval, her acceptance. I wanted her to at least be happy for me. But, Dawn was right, as usual.

"You know, my job used to be valuing the opinion of others. It's hard to turn off sometimes," I joked, and I leaned my head on her shoulder. She put her arm around my waist and squeezed.

"I get it, Chellie." She leaned her head on top of mine. "But now, only the opinion of one person matters. Well, two people: yours and Tanner's."

"You're right."

"I know."

"I shouldn't have let my mother wind me up like that."

"That woman is chaotic." She laughed, and I joined her. "And what is the deal with her new hostage, I mean, husband?" We laughed even harder.

"Don't know. Don't care." I shrugged. "And the few times I've spoken to her in the last few months, she keeps asking me when I'm going to come to my senses and go back to work with Brenda. So, we don't talk about Richard." I sighed. "Are your mom and Sunny enjoying the party?"

"My mom is enjoying the food," she chuckled. "She's happy to be heading to the dance floor without her cane. And my sister is schmoozing with all of the surgeons and doctors." Dawn's mother had Multiple Sclerosis, and her sister was in medical school.

"How's real-life Grey's Anatomy working out for Sunny?" I asked with a grin.

"Apparently, there's not as many random hook-ups in closets, and—hey, it looks like you can ask her yourself."

I looked up to see my grandmother and Dawn's little sister rumbling towards us in a golf cart. Nana was behind the wheel, and Sunny rode shotgun.

We scrambled to our feet as they approached us.

"Hey, Chellie," Sunny said with a big grin as she folded me into her arms. I didn't do the best job of returning her hug because I still held the pile of Tanner's clothes. She glanced at the crumpled tuxedo and then into the woods and back at me. "Is he out there right now...as a bear?" she asked in an excited whisper before craning her neck, possibly hoping to catch a glimpse of my grumpy boyfriend's furry alter ego. Sonny was just as accepting as Dawn when I told her about Tanner being a shifter but also a lot more curious. I nodded and smiled. "So cool," she said before she turned her attention to her sister. "Hey, D, I think Mom's getting a little tired. We should probably take her back to the city."

"Is she okay? We just got here." Dawn asked with alarm. Sunny put her arm around her shoulder and turned her in the direction of the house.

"She's fine. I just think she overdid it with the two-step and the caviar."

"Here, dear." Nana handed Sunny the keys to the golf cart. "I'm going to walk back."

"Are you sure, Nana Woods?" Dawn asked.

"Yes." Nana patted her cheek and nodded. "I could use the solitude. It's a little crowded in there." She tilted her head at the house in the distance. The sisters nodded and climbed into the cart.

"How are you doing out here?" Nana asked and stroked my face, brushing away a tear as we watched the golf cart disappear.

"I feel terrible. Tanner and I have fought before, but this is the first time I'm really worried," I confessed.

"If you were interested in some unsolicited advice," Nana pulled the pile of clothes from my arms and gently set it on the ground at the base of the tree before clasping both of my hands, "I would tell you: do not let anyone come between you and true happiness. I would give anything— except for you and your mother, of course— to be with Henry again. I let our families come between us. I let money come between us. And I do not want that for you. I see how happy Tanner makes you. I see how happy you make him. Hold onto that. Never ever let it go." She folded me in her arms and squeezed. Her hug opened the floodgates. I shook in her arms, and I sobbed. Nana shushed me and stroked my hair while I cried for what felt like hours but was probably several minutes.

"Well, aren't you beautiful?" my grandmother whispered. She couldn't have been talking about me because I must have looked like a mess. Not wearing waterproof mascara when I knew I'd have an interaction with my mother was a rookie mistake, but Nana was looking at something over my shoulder. I picked my head up to see. A giant black bear with a tan muzzle and sad eyes stood on all fours a few feet away from us.

My bear.

My grandmother approached him slowly and cautiously with her hand outstretched. Tanner lowered his head and allowed her to smooth a palm over the downy fur between his ears. She gave him a few gentle pats before she backed away, smiling. Her eyes were glossy with unshed tears.

"Well." She pressed her hands together and smiled at us, but I could sense the profound sadness in her expression. "I'm going to get back to my guests. I'm sure you two have a lot to discuss, and I'm assuming that when you change, there will be a lot of things you don't want me to see." She indicated Tanner's discarded tuxedo with a mischievous smile.

"Nana?!" I gasped. She winked at me and turned to make the long, slow walk back to the house.

As I watched her walk away, Tanner nudged me in the back with his warm, wet nose, and I wrapped my arm around his head to gently scratch his chin. "Feel better, handsome?" I whispered softly. "Are you ready to talk to me now?"

———— •••• ————

TANNER SAT against the trunk of the tree, wearing his boxer briefs and his T-shirt. He cradled my head in his lap and gently stroked my hair. We still hadn't spoken since we left the party, but I could tell he wasn't angry anymore; well, not as angry. Shifting seemed to have that effect on him. He once told me that letting his bear take his skin eased his human mind and put his worries into perspective.

Tanner stroked my face and gently curled his index finger around my chin to turn my head so I could look into his eyes.

"Chellie," he said in a low, stern voice. "You're my mate. Mine. *I* take care of *you*."

I opened my mouth to protest, but he pressed a calloused fingertip over my lips.

"But, I am also *your* mate, and it will take some getting used to, but I know that sometimes you'll want to take care of me, too. I never want anything or anybody to come between us. Not money, not our families, and definitely not my *stubborn pride*." He smiled down at me.

"You were listening." It wasn't a question, and I furrowed my brow at him with a small smirk.

"I wasn't eavesdropping. I'm a bear, sweetheart." His beard twitched at me. "I hear everything." He leaned down to kiss me, and I met him halfway. "I have a question."

"Ask away," I said and reached up to stroke his face.

"Are you ashamed that I'm not rich?" His eyes were soft with worry, and it made my heart clench.

I bolted upright and turned my whole body to face him, cupping his face in my hands.

"I could never be ashamed of you. Tanner, you're the best thing that's ever happened to me. You've given me more happiness than I've ever seen or ever thought was possible. The kind of love you give me, the kind of love I found with you, for you, and the way you've taught me to love myself is priceless. I would only be ashamed if I have ever said or did anything to make you feel otherwise." I pressed my lips to his, and my eyes prickled with tears.

"I'm so sorry for what happened back there. I just wanted my mother to know how proud I am of you and the lodges. How ready I am to share my life with you. You've opened your heart and home to me, and I want to do the same. If you'll let me..."

His expression was unreadable, and he seemed to be deep in thought. Just when I was about to die from anticipation, he looked at me and nodded.

The wave of relief that hit me was so strong that I let out a small sob, and a tear rolled down my cheek. Tanner wiped it away with his thumb and captured my mouth with his. I tightened my arms around his neck and kissed him like my life depended on it.

"I guess you weren't exaggerating about your mother," he chuckled when our mouths finally separated. "I almost miss the mountain lion."

"She is definitely the worst. I promise you, we won't have to see her again...until next year, I guess," I said, indicating the party.

"I love you, Chellie." He wrapped his arms around my waist and pulled me into his lap. "If you want to use your money to renovate the lodges, I'm okay with that, but I want to make it official. I want contracts, and I want this to be a partnership. I want us to build the resort together. And I don't want you keeping secrets from me."

"That's exactly what I want, baby, and from now on, I'm an open book." I repositioned myself so I straddled him and wrapped my arms around his neck, pulling our mouths together. "Can you turn down the He-Man stuff? I love how much you love me, but I'm no wilting flower, remember? I'm an ax-wielding badass who escaped a mountain lion attack and dragged a 250-pound man into a cabin."

"Yes, you are." He grinned and kissed me. "I'm a very lucky man."

"Yes, you are." I smiled and scrunched my nose at him.

"I can't completely turn down the He-Man stuff." He brushed a stray lock of hair away from my forehead. "But I promise, I'll try?" He rolled his lips between his teeth and raised his eyebrows, and I knew that was as good as I was getting.

"Close enough. Do you know what I want now?"

"No, but I get the feeling you're going to tell me." His mouth twitched with a little smirk, and I narrowed my eyes at him. I released my hands from his neck and started to pull the skirt of my gown up to my hips, gently rocking my bare sex against his erection. Our only barrier was the thin fabric of his boxer briefs. "You didn't wear underwear to the party?"

"I did. You took them off, remember?" I pressed my forehead to his and rubbed our noses together.

"Oh, yeah." He reached between us and freed his cock from his briefs, giving it slow, lazy strokes with his palm. "I did, didn't I?"

I answered him with a kiss and raised myself on my knees before slowly lowering myself onto his shaft and rocking back and forth.

"Mmmmmm," I murmured as he reached under my dress to palm the globes of my ass. He slipped the tip of his finger into the puckered bud between my cheeks, causing me to whimper and ride him even harder.

"Oh, God, right there. Yes. Just like that." I bounced up and down on his hips even more furiously until I felt a shiver of ecstasy wash over me like a warm wave. I threw my head back and grunted through my release. Tanner laid me down on the warm ground and took me again, pumping furiously in and out of me until he came, growling the word *mine* over and over again while planting little kisses on my throat and jaw. He grazed his teeth over the bite mark he gave me, marking me as his.

He collapsed next to me on the ground and covered me with his tuxedo jacket. I repositioned my body, so my head rested on his chest, and we stared at the sky.

"Can you believe we've only been together for a few months?" I asked.

"No," he replied. "It feels like a lot longer."

"What?!" I picked my head up, and he chuckled, pressing me back on to his chest.

"In the best possible way, baby." He planted a kiss on the top of my head.

"Good." I snuggled closer. "Do you want to go back to the party?"

"Do I have to put my pants back on?"

"I don't think Nana or Marissa would mind if you didn't, but yes, you do," I said in a giggle.

"Eh." I felt him shrug. "I could stay out here for a little while longer," he said with a contented sigh and tightened his arm around my waist.

So, that's what we did.

THE END

THE SOUNDTRACK
BEAR WITH ME

The Bear with Me playlist can be found on Spotify

1. JOSHUA - DOLLY PARTON

2. SUCKER - JONAS BROTHERS

3. TRAMPOLINE - SHAED

4. BAD GUY - BILLIE EILISH

5. EASTSIDE (WITH HALSEY & KHALID) - BENNY BLANCO

6. BREAK UP WITH YOUR GIRLFRIEND - ARIANA GRANDE

7. HONEY - MARIAH CAREY

8. BOOGIE OOGIE OOGIE - A TASTE OF HONEY

9. CIRCLES - POST MALONE

10. HOT GIRL BUMMER - BLACKBEAR

11. SOMEONE YOU LOVED - LEWIS CAPALDI

12. BEAUTIFUL PEOPLE - ED SHEERAN (FEATURING KHALID)

13. MOTIVATION - NORMANI

14. TRUTH HURTS - LIZZO

15. HOW DO YOU SLEEP - SAM SMITH

Playlist link: bit.ly/BearWithMeSongs

AUTHOR'S NOTE

Dearest Reader,

Thank you for reading Bear with Me.

This book was originally inspired by the Dolly Parton song "Joshua" and is a sequel to Resolutions.

Thank you:

My amazing critique partner, Marina Garcia. I wrote this book, largely, in part to our nightly writing sprint marathons. I could not have finished this book or Everything's Better with Lisa without you.

My amazing beta readers who gave me amazing feed back and the confidence in my tiny little story.

Tasha L. Harrison for creating our weekly write ins and for always pushing me to be a better storyteller. I'm getting there. Your ingenuity and encouragement continues to inspire me and I am so lucky to know you.

Katrina Jackson for loving this story & pushing me to go further.

Thank you, Miri Stone for your inexhaustible shifter knowledge. Your inspiration, critiques and insights made me believe I could write a paranormal romantic comedy.

Rhonda Merwarth for squeezing my teeny tiny book into your crazy schedule at the last minute. When I thought my story was perfect you pushed me to make it better & it worked. Thank you for being the other half of my brain, sexy Darth Vader.

Kai, thank you for being my right & left hand and editing Grin & Bear It with less than a day's notice. You're a rock star!

Hellhoneyy, as always, for bringing my characters to life with your vivid drawings.

My ARC team for giving their time and energy to read my work and help spread the word.

Thank you so much, dear reader, for reading Bear with Me! I hope you liked it. Please consider leaving a review on Goodreads or wherever you share your good news!

PS If you loved Chellie & Tanner's story & want to share the love via social media, here's a link to some promo images you can use: bit.ly/PROMOBWM

Don't forget to tag me: @lucyedenauthor on facebook, instagram & twitter, because I'm nosy.

October 2019 & October 2020

xoxo,

lucy

ALSO BY LUCY EDEN

DON'T MISS MY NEXT RELEASE!

Sign up for my newsletter for updates & freebies.

VISIT LUCYEDEN.COM

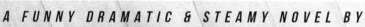

A FUNNY DRAMATIC & STEAMY NOVEL BY
LUCY EDEN

"I'VE READ THIS ALREADY. BE JEALOUS."
- JODIE SLAUGHTER
AUTHOR OF WHITE WHISKEY BARGAIN

EVERYTHING'S
better
WITH LISA

ONE
COLE

2-6-5-3. Red X.

"Fuck!"

2-6-5-3. Red X.

"Shit!"

I typed my code into the keypad a third time with no success.

"Goddammit!" I kicked the wood doorframe of the hundred-year-old Harlem brownstone I'd called home for the past six years.

"Hey, asshole! Shut the fuck up!" a female voice shouted from the ground-level apartment.

I looked over the banister to see a short woman with waist-length, chestnut-colored hair staring up at me, holding a baseball bat.

"Crystal?" It was too dark to see her clearly. I was definitely more than a little buzzed, and my biological mother was the only short woman with long dark brown hair I knew. But why was she holding a baseball bat, and why was her voice different?

With a little difficulty, I walked down the stairs to get a closer look. The woman took a step back as I approached and held the bat higher, tightening her grip on the neck.

"My name is not Crystal, and I live here."

Upon closer inspection—as close as I could get without getting clocked in the head, anyway—I could tell she definitely wasn't Crystal. She was younger, way more beautiful, and she didn't have my birth mother's bright blue eyes. Crystal also moved back to Missouri four years ago. Most importantly, tiny Babe Ruth definitely didn't live in my house. I was drunk, but not that drunk.

"You live in here?" That wasn't exactly how I meant to phrase that, but my brain and my mouth weren't cooperating. Also, I'd become aware that I was leaning against the brick wall of the stoop to support my weight.

"Yes," gorgeous, not-Crystal hissed. "I live here." She was so sincere that I was hit with a wave of confusion, and when it ebbed, realization slapped me in the face. I took a step back and looked up at the door I had been kicking a moment ago, then I looked to the right at the door I should've been kicking.

"Shit." I did it again. I went to the wrong fucking house.

Why did these brownstones all look the same?

I turned to head to the brownstone where my code would work, and I guess I turned too fast because I stumbled and had to grab the railing to keep from crashing to the ground.

"Are you okay?" She lowered her bat, but she didn't take a step forward. I was drunk. I was trying to enter the wrong house, and I had almost busted my ass in front of my sexy neighbor.

"I'm fine, *Crystal*. Mind your business." This ordeal was embarrassing enough without Batgirl, suddenly concerned for my welfare.

Hadn't she just called me an asshole?

I didn't need her help. I was a grown-ass man who needed to walk twenty feet to his front door.

"Excuse me?" she said. "Again, dickhead, my name is not Crystal, and you screaming in the middle of the night woke me up from my much-needed sleep, so it is my business."

I turned to face her and felt myself sway as I tried to stabilize. Her outburst was sexy as fuck and I felt an overwhelming urge to kiss her.

Nope. Nope.

That was definitely the alcohol talking.

I can't kiss her.

I have to get home.

The word *home* floated to my consciousness, but instead of focusing on that goal, I decided to speak.

"You kind of look like my mother, but not really. Her name is Crystal. I'm fine. Just got confused. My house looks exactly like my sister's house." I pointed at the brownstone next door before pointing at Kimmy's.

"Your sister?" She gave me the look, the skeptical look I get when I tell people about my family. One would think I'd gotten used to it after all these years. Maybe it was all the tequila shots, but tonight it pissed me off. She continued, "The woman that owns this brownstone is not your sister, and I'm not your mother, so you need to take your drunk ass home, to your actual house, before I call the cops."

"Kimbery Shimmins is my shishter!" I yelled as I backed away from her towards my house. I could hear myself slurring my words and considered the possibility that trying to walk and talk at the same time wasn't the best idea. I turned toward my house, continuing to amble forward. "And I'm glad you're not my mom because my mom is awesome, and you'd be a shitty mom with your baseball bat and your potty mouth."

Even though I was sure I just used the words "potty mouth," I knew I'd said something profound because I was met with silence.

I turned to look at her and found her expression blank. A loud and expletive-filled response was what I expected, but she just stood there, frozen and a little sad. A feeling like regret crept over me, but I couldn't figure out what I should have felt regretful about. I tried to replay the last thing I said, but I couldn't fucking remember, something about Kimberly and a shitty potty?

That look... I couldn't stand seeing it, so I turned away from her and climbed the steps to my door, where I typed in the four-digit code.

Green checkmark.

———— •••• ————

THE THROBBING in my head woke me up before I could open my eyes. I'd stayed out late drinking last night and stumbled into bed fully clothed. Again. I barely remembered anything after Beck Cameron's last round of shots. I must have taken a cab home, and I vaguely remembered meeting someone last night. A woman—a beautiful woman who was pissed at me for some reason. I climbed out of bed and trudged to the bathroom, swallowed two Advil, and turned on the shower.

The hot water beat me into consciousness, and memories of last night began to float together in tiny little patches. I had tried to get into Kimberly's house last night, thinking it was mine. We used to have the codes to each other's houses until I went to her home by accident one night, and her fiancé almost beat the shit out of me with a hammer before he realized who I was. The thought ignited a flicker of a memory. The beautiful woman I met last night had a baseball bat. She was outside of Kimberly's house. I said something to upset her, but I couldn't remember what it was. I focused on putting myself together and getting to work.

———— • • • • ————

AFTER A STOP AT STARBUCKS, I stepped off of the elevator at seven forty-five. Technically the offices didn't open until eight thirty, and unless we were working on a big case, the senior associates and partners usually didn't show up until after nine. I was a first-year associate, which meant I always had to be here, working my ass off, but not busy, in case one of the partners needed something. My father was also a partner at this law firm before he became a judge, so I also had to prove that I wasn't just a rich kid using Daddy's connections. My dream had always been to work for Hollander and Cameron ever since my dad would bring me here as a kid. I wanted to be just like him. Whenever Crystal was in trouble, we would come to this building, and her lawyer, Reginald Simmons, would fix everything like a superhero. He was also a legend at the firm and was now a United States district court judge, so I'm sure my presence at the firm wasn't purely based on merit. That's why I was determined to work twice as hard as everyone else.

"Good Morning, Judy." I flashed the office manager a grin and handed her a venti mocha latte, 130 degrees.

"Thank you, Cole." She snatched the cup from me and took a sip. "There is not enough coffee in the world. Did I ever tell you how much I love you?"

"Every day, but I never get tired of hearing it," I called over my shoulder. I sat at my desk, or a fancy version of a cubicle, and started working.

In the years I spent daydreaming about being an attorney, I thought it would be closer to *Law and Order* and not hours sorting through discovery requests, filing motions, and reading depositions for hours. It would be worth it if the work were fulfilling. I wanted to become a lawyer to help people like Crystal and me. Most of what we did at Hollander and Cameron involved helping rich people get richer.

Discovery requests in the movies usually depicted someone running into a conference room carrying a file that held the one piece of paper that was the key to winning the "big case." In reality, discovery requests could be four boxes of documents that need to be combed through carefully to find a specific piece of information that may or may not be there. This was a task for first-years. Most of my morning was spent sifting through three years of email conversations from a real estate company looking for any mention of steel beams.

"There he is," Beck Cameron called behind me. He was the son of Bryce Cameron, one of the managing partners. He'd have a good shot at following in his father's footsteps if he wasn't such a fuckup. Beck's voice was still raspy from last night. "How the fuck do you do it?"

I turned to face him. He was in the same suit he wore to work yesterday, a pair of sunglasses, and sipped something green out of a giant clear Starbucks cup.

"You look like shit."

"I feel like shit." He dropped into his chair.

"Are those the clothes you had on yesterday, man?" They smelled like last night too.

"Well, I didn't exactly make it home yesterday." He dropped his sunglasses and raised his eyebrows. "If you know what I mean..."

"You mean, you met someone at the bar last night and went to their house to have sex," I deadpanned.

His expression soured. "Maybe if you tried it once in a while, you'd be in a better mood."

"I'll think about it." I turned back to my computer.

I ignored Beck and tried to focus on work, but the only thing I could think about was my bat-wielding neighbor.

———————— • • • • ————————

IT WAS a quarter to nine when I finally stepped off of the subway to make the five-minute walk to my house. My parents lived in the brownstone on the corner. I saw that the front parlor light was on, and my stomach had the Pavlovian response it usually did whenever I got in proximity to my mom's kitchen. The growling also reminded me that I worked straight through lunch and skipped dinner.

Walking into my parents' house was a crapshoot. Mom and Dad were always affectionate growing up, but since the three of us moved out... Well, it was always a good idea to announce yourself when you came in.

"Mom? Dad?" I yelled after taking off my shoes and walking into the empty sitting room.

"We're in here, baby," Mom called. It sounded like she was in the dining room.

The faint melody of Marvin Gaye's "What's Going On" played as I found my parents sitting on opposite sides of the table wearing their reading glasses and hunched over laptops, probably working on real estate stuff. Dad was a judge, and Mom was a psychiatrist, but together, they had invested in real estate around New York since the early nineties, and most of their money came from those properties. It was how their three kids were able to afford their own brownstones on the same street.

"Are you just getting home from work?" Mom asked as I kissed her on the cheek. I nodded and loosened my tie. "That's ridiculous." She grabbed my cheeks, tipped my head to the side as if she were inspecting me for damage. "Look at this luggage under your eyes. Are you getting enough sleep?"

"Beverly, leave that boy alone." Dad closed his laptop, removed his glasses, and pinched the bridge of his nose, squinting.

"They are working him too hard. Look at his face." She was still gripping my chin. She forced me to look at my dad.

"Please. My easiest day as a public defender was worse than my hardest day at HC, and I had lives depending on me. He'll be fine." Then he muttered, "He'd be better if he stopped staying out late after work and took his butt home at a decent hour."

It was time for me to make my exit.

"Where was all this sympathy when I was working all those late hours?" he asked.

"You are not my child, and if memory serves me correctly, and it always does, I took care of you plenty..." She released me and eyed my father suggestively.

"You still do," he replied in a voice too deep for my comfort.

It was really time for me to make my exit.

I cleared my throat to remind them I was still in the room. Mom laughed and patted my face.

"Go in the kitchen and fix yourself a plate. Kimmy is in there, so you better hurry if you want some corn."

I swung the kitchen door open to find my sister scooping the last of the corn out of a large bowl and dividing it between two plates.

"Hey, Stringbean." I took the bowl from her and managed to salvage some of the corn. The salty, buttery smell made my stomach growl again. "You opening a soup kitchen?"

"No," she said and tried to snatch the bowl back before I held it out of her reach. "Adam's working late, and I'm making him a plate."

Adam was Kimberly's fiancé. They'd only been together for a few months, but he was a good guy and made her happy.

"I thought he was in Barbados." I clutched the bowl while I reached for a plate.

"He is, but he had some meetings in New York, and Vittoria can't fly anymore. So, we're both in the same place at the same time for a few days." Her face spread in a wistful grin and she started scooping baked mac and cheese onto the plates.

My sister was the executive assistant to the head of the real estate and hospitality division of Wolfe Industries, a Fortune 50 company. Usually, she was jet-setting around the world, but her boss was in the latter part of her pregnancy and couldn't fly, so she was home more often. Adam was an architect and was building a luxury resort in Barbados for Wolfe. He flew back and forth a lot and was preparing to move there for the foreseeable future. Long-distance relationships were supposed to be hard, but these two seemed to make it work. I wasn't a fan of long relationships, much less long-distance ones.

My sister and I managed to divide the leftover meat-loaf and cornbread without coming to blows, though she took all four corner pieces. We were wrapping our plates in foil when I remembered last night's encounter.

"Hey, do you have a tenant?"

She froze. "Yeah," she answered in a slow, cautious tone. "Why?" She turned to face me, eyeing me with suspicion.

"How long has she lived there?"

"She moved in about eight months ago. Again, why?"

"She's lived there for eight months, and I've never seen her?"

"No." She shook her head and went back to covering her plates.

"No, what?" I asked, knowing exactly what she was protesting and trying to stifle a grin.

"Stay away from her. She's sweet. She minds her own business, and she always pays her rent on time."

"Excuse me? Your sweet tenant who minds her own business tried to attack me with a baseball bat last night."

She whipped around to face me.

"What? That doesn't sound like—" She almost said her name, then stopped herself. "Why did she try to attack you with a bat?"

"I might have accidentally tried to get into the wrong house last night." I shrugged and reached for the cake dish.

"Again, Cole?" She glared at me and dug her fist into her hip.

"*Yes, Kimberly,*" I mimicked her. "You know all of the houses look the same at night."

"And when you're drunk?" She tilted her head and raised her eyebrows.

"I am a social drinker. I work ten-hour, high-stress days, then I have a few drinks with some of the other associates after work. It's networking. It's an important part of my job."

She narrowed her eyes and pursed her lips, mimicking Mom's *you're so full of shit* face. "You really need to get your shit together, Cole." She turned and started slicing into the yellow cake with chocolate frosting.

"You know what, Kimmy? You're the last one who should be lecturing me about facing hard truths."

"And what the hell is that supposed to mean?" She turned to face me, but she was still holding the knife.

"Put the knife down, and I'll tell you."

She looked down at her hand, snorted, and dropped the knife on the counter.

"Where are you taking those plates?"

Her smile dissolved, and she hesitated before answering me, not meeting my eye. "To Adam's apartment. So..."

"When's the last time he stayed at your place?"

"We're not in court, Cole. Could you get to the point?"

"He's still acting weird about the brownstone and the fact that you have more money than he does."

"You're ridiculous. It's none of your business, and Adam is just more comfortable at his place. I love his apartment, and I love him, and we're hardly in the same place long enough for it to become an issue. And now that's settled. But let me reiterate that I want you to leave my tenant alone. She's been through a lot, and she's not your type."

"What do you mean she's been through a lot?"

"Again, none of your business." She'd finished piling and packing her plates and was sliding them into one of the five hundred plastic shopping bags Mom kept in the cabinet under the sink.

"And what do you mean she's not my type? What the hell is my type?"

"The type of woman who steals your sister's jewelry when you invite her over for family dinner…"

"That happened once."

"Or the type of woman that proclaims at a family barbecue that she didn't know Black families could adopt white children."

"That was a different chick, and in my defense, she seemed a lot smarter when I met her."

"Bye, Cole." She was already leaving the kitchen. "Leave my tenant alone and fix your life."

"Love you too, sis!" I yelled at her retreating form.

She stopped, sighed, and turned to me.

"I'm sorry for all the shit I just said. You're amazing, Fruity Pebbles, but you have horrible taste in women, and your current life choices are questionable."

"You really suck at apologizing. You know that?" I cracked a smile, and she chuckled. "So, I'm amazing but still not good enough for your sweet, bat-wielding tenant?"

She heaved a sigh. "Look, I'm not at liberty to share her personal business, but I don't think it's a good idea."

"For her or for me?"

"For either one of you."

———————— • • • • ————————

THANK you for reading this bonus chapter of Everything's Better with Lisa. Visit <u>lucyeden.com</u>

ABOUT THE AUTHOR

Lucy Eden is the *nom de plume* of a romance obsessed author who writes the kind of romance she loves to read. She's a sucker for alphas with a soft gooey center, over the top romantic gestures, strong & smart MCs, humor, love at first sight (or pretty damn close), happily ever afters & of course, steamy love scenes.

When Lucy isn't writing, she's busy reading—or listening to—every book she can get her hands on—romance or otherwise.

She lives in New York with her husband, two children, a turtle & a Yorkshire Terrier.

facebook.com/lucyedenauthor

twitter.com/lucyedenauthor

instagram.com/lucyedenauthor

bookbub.com/authors/lucy-eden

goodreads.com/lucyedenauthor

pinterest.com/lucyedenromance

Lightning Source UK Ltd.
Milton Keynes UK
UKHW021224171220
375421UK00008B/450